Front Pivot

Chris Boucher

A Wings ePress, Inc.
Young Adult Novel

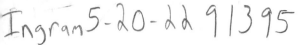

Ingram 5-20-22 91395

YA
FIC
Boucher

Wings ePress, Inc.

Edited by: Jeanne Smith
Copy Edited by: Brian Hatfield
Executive Editor: Jeanne Smith
Cover Artist: Trisha FitzGerald-Jung
Cover image: Pixabay

Wings ePress Books
www.wingsepress.com

Copyright © 2021 by: Chris Boucher
ISBN-13: 978-1-61309-531-7

Published In the United States Of America

Wings ePress Inc.
3000 N. Rock Road
Newton, KS 67114

What They Are Saying About

Front Pivot

Chris excelled during his time in the Master's Creative Writing Program at Southern New Hampshire University, so I'm not surprised to see he has now published his second novel since earning his degree. I'm sure it helped that he worked on both during his studies and received invaluable support from instructors, peers, and support staff. I'm eager to see where he goes from here!

—Andrea Morrow, M.Ed., Academic Advisor at SNHU

I have loved basketball since I started playing in 1958 while growing up on the South Side of Chicago. I have also enjoyed sports books where basketball is part of the story. *Front Pivot* is the second in the *Pivot* series, both of which I have enjoyed. Exploring the challenges that a young boy faces who has basketball as a major part of his life rings true to my background and I enjoyed the way *Front Pivot* skillfully uses basketball to tell a substantive family story that explores serious, contemporary issues. I'm ready for the next installment in the series!

—Bill Campbell, Comedian

Noel Prince searches for answers to puzzling problems in this coming-of-age novel. Some are relatively simple, such as how to make the high school basketball team and learning how to deal with other students. Some are more complex, such as why his older brother left town and trying to understand his late father's confusing actions while serving in Afghanistan. Noel's tenacity drops him into the middle of a nefarious event that also proves enlightening in his search for answers. Boucher's novel is entertaining and informative on several levels, one that will captivate readers until the very end and make them look forward to the next book in the *Pivot* series.

—Michael Embry, author of *The Bully List* and *Shooting Star*

Dedication

For Fred
***

One

Let's make history together, the president's tweet goes. *Avenge the Mouse! And this time we'll finish the job!!*

I hit the power button on my phone to make the screen go black as soon as my spidey-sense tells me Old Testament is shoulder-surfing behind me. It's like a reflex of mine. What can I say? I like my privacy.

Not that there's much to fear at home these days. With Pax gone, it's just me and my gramps in the condo, and since he won't wear his specs unless he's watching one of his TV shows, I'm pretty sure he can't read what's on my phone anyway. Plus, what my boy Boyd calls my Sideshow Bob dreads give me a little extra cover, too.

Too bad the tweet won't leave my head as easy as it left my screen. If only Coach hadn't made us follow the president's Twitter feed for his English class. Or that he never made the jump from the Y to Holloway High. He takes everything too seriously—first hoops, now school, where is it gonna end?

OT drops next to me on the couch and my cushion starts to sink in his direction. I have to plant my feet against the floor to avoid sliding right into him.

"Noel, you're acting awful suspicious lately," he turns his round face to me and booms in my ear. With his little hook nose, he looks kind of like an owl, and he projects his voice like one, too. It's a little too close for comfort, almost like he's inside my head.

"If you're worrying about your brother, stop. Pascal is not about to do anything stupid. He's about as responsible as an eighteen-year-old can get, just like I raised him."

"Yeah, I know," I say, not believing a word of what I'm saying. Responsible is not what I'd call someone who picked now—of all times—to take a gap year. Yup, he's taking a year off between high school and college to do...nothing. Right when the president wants to get his war on.

My bro should be the one reading these tweet storms! The stuff the guy comes up with is crazy. He definitely lost it—a ways back. If he starts the draft again like he's threatening to do, Pax is screwed.

Not that he's worried about it. I'm starting to think he's looking for trouble. I caught him studying what I'm thinking is our dad's war journal, and then he up and takes off. He says he's heading to Florida to take a break. That seems like the last place you'd want to be right now, especially after what the terrorists did to Magicland with their October Surprise.

Pax said he couldn't resist the cheap flights. *They're cheap for a reason, fool!*

I think he's got a hero complex. Our dad got a Bronze Star in Afghanistan and everyone says he's a big war hero. And in case we forget it, we see the actual medal every day. It's right there in our hallway Hall of Fame, framed in gold, just like his obituary.

So Pax feels like he has to measure up. The thing is, he's already a legend of his own around here! He took Holloway High to the state championship last year, basically all by himself. I think that's the real reason he's taking a gap year. Despite all he did, he didn't get any offers from D1 schools. He got plenty from Division 2 and 3 schools, but apparently those weren't good enough for him, so he decided to wait it out.

"You got all you need for school?" OT goes off again and I almost jump out of my shoes. Maybe if he actually had his glasses on, he'd realize how close we are. Whatever. At least it's a reminder that I need to hit him up for some new kicks.

"Almost." I turn and give him my million-dollar smile. "I just need one more thing—a pair of Adapt BBs."

"Them fancy sneakers? I told you, you can get a pair of those when you make it to the NBA. And the shoe company gives them to you for free!"

"I'm not gonna have a shot at the NBA if I can't even make my high school team. And what if I need those sneakers to do it?" I try to smile even brighter, making my teeth glint like you see on TV. Too bad it doesn't work, because I don't hear a ding to go with it.

"Well, I like the Bs in the name, I'll say that." He returns my smile with his own go-to look, an expressionless game face. "Cuz you know you have to get at least Bs to go out for that team."

"I'm doing good so far," I say, and I believe that. The first semester is almost up and I feel like I'm on track. But people always tell me I'm too cocky for my own good, so there's that, too. And then there's Coach. I've got him for homeroom, English, and Social Studies, and with his weird motivational techniques, you never really know where you stand. Just when you start to feel comfortable, trouble is usually right around the corner.

"Just keep working as hard at school as you do at basketball," OT says. "And things will take care of themselves."

Really? When do things ever take care of themselves? If they did, would I be living with my gramps right now? Nothing against OT, but wouldn't I be better off if I had a mom and a dad? How about a mom or a dad? Because I don't have either and haven't had either for about as long as I can remember.

OT must feel my doubt because he actually stops to explain himself. "What I'm saying is, work hard and you'll get the grades I want and them fancy sneakers you want."

You know he's working hard himself, because he actually closes with something like a real smile. As close as he gets anyway. Problem is, he has no idea what he's talking about. Ballin' these days is a lot more than just playing at the Y. This is high school and the basketball is legit. You have to look like you belong, too, and those kicks are as tight as my handle.

"Since we're on the subject." It's OT again. "You know I'm on my way back to church for the elders' meeting. What you gonna do with yourself this afternoon?"

"I've got some homework to do, then I'm meeting Wick at the Y. We're gonna work on our games."

I've got homework to do all right. But it's nothing I can get to while OT is home.

"That's what I'm talking about," he says. "You got your business lined up the right way. And good company. I like that kid Wick. He's got his priorities in the right order."

Of course he likes Wick. I haven't met an adult who doesn't. His IQ is off the charts. And so are his grades. But I don't care about any of that right now. I'm all about his basketball IQ. And the two of us, unlike Pax, actually do have something to prove.

OT gets up, satisfied with my plan. He heads to the door, gives me a nod, then goes out, closes it behind him, and locks it tight.

I'm home alone now—time to step to that homework of mine.

Two

I get up from the couch and slide past the windows, checking to make sure OT didn't forget something and decide to come back for it. Once I'm sure I'm home free, I head up the stairs and into my bro's room.

It's dark because all the shades are closed, as usual. I leave them alone—the fewer things I touch in here the better—and turn on the flashlight on my phone so I can see. It's not like me to slink around like this, but it's just something I have to do.

I go straight to his desk, which only takes a few steps because the big old thing takes up about a third of the room. It's solid wood and weighs a ton. It used to be my gram's. She worked as a secretary for something like fifty years, and when she retired, they gave it to her as a gift. I guess they thought she'd miss it. When me and Pax moved in, their den became his room and since there was no one around who could move it, it stayed right here.

It takes all I've got to open the drawer I need to get to, the top one on the left. It's heavy and stuck fast. I set my feet and pull the handle with both hands until it finally opens with a pop. I shine my flashlight deep inside and see exactly what I'm looking for—a little green book sitting all by itself in the back compartment.

I reach in and pick it up. The vinyl jacket is faded and worn out and feels kind of slick. The cracked gold lettering on the cover only says *One Year Journal*. It's enough. I know my dad spent a year in Afghanistan back in the day. I wasn't even born then. This thing is older than me, but only by a little. Still, it feels like more like a century.

There's a lock on the journal but the band has been cut. Whether Pax did that or not, I can't say. For all I know, my dad lost the key and did it himself. So I go ahead and crack it open—literally. The pages actually make a sound when I separate them. They smell dusty and are all stiff and yellow with stains.

Part of the damage has to be my dad's blood, sweat, and tears from all he went through. And with my clammy hands, I'm probably adding to the mix. When Pax is the one who should be sweating!

I pick a random page near the middle and start reading:

Left KOP this afternoon and went outside the wire. Patrolled what was basically a rocky dirt trail running between incredibly steep hills—all in full gear. What a slog!

After we returned to the outpost, received word a convoy was hit in Ambush Alley. Organized QRF to help. When we got there the battle was well underway. An IED flipped a Humvee onto its roof. The explosion also blew off its doors and up armor, which lay on the ground all around it. A couple of RPG rounds whooshed past and the sound of gunfire was everywhere.

It was getting dark and we couldn't see much. I just aimed at the muzzle flashes I saw behind the rocks and trees. I hope I didn't hit anyone. I just wanted the shooting to stop.

Apaches finally came in and cleared everyone out. We threw smoke grenades and returned to the outpost.

My mouth was dry as sandpaper during the fight and my clothes were wringing wet from sweat. I was shaky and nervous and had a sick feeling in my stomach the whole time.

A couple of guys needed medevac, but Larry and I were all right. I was happy to get back in one piece. I've never been so glad to see a day end.

A rap at the front door brings me back to the condo. I head over to the shade and take a peek outside. A delivery guy dressed in brown drops a package on the steps, then spins and goes back to his truck. I better get downstairs and grab what he left before someone else gets to it. In this neighborhood, we got all kinds of porch pirates.

Before I'm done with the journal, I take a closer look at some scribbles on the sides of the pages. The handwriting is different from the rest of it, and it seems kind of familiar. I'm guessing Pax is adding his own notes to what he's reading:

KOP—Korengal Outpost
QRF—Quick Reaction Force
IED—Improvised Explosive Device
Humvee—High Mobility Multipurpose Wheeled Vehicle
Up armor—Extra armor added to Humvees to improve
     protection
RPG—Rocket Propelled Grenade
Apache—Attack helicopter
Medevac—Medical evacuation
Nice job Dad—Finally some action!

So I was right. My big bro is going through this thing—word by word. He's studying it hard. I've seen him hunched over it a few times and every time my view was interrupted by a door closing in my face. I never asked what he was doing, but somehow, I kind of knew anyway.

The worst part is, if he left without the journal, he must have finished reading it. Which means his studies are over. And it's time for action. On top of the action my dad already saw.

I snap the book shut and put it back where I found it. As the drawer creaks to a close, I feel some notes of my own form in my head:

Why you going through this now, bro? I thought you were taking time off from studying!

And don't you think OT is right? Isn't one hero in a family enough?

Three

The sun goes right for my eyes when I step out the door, blazing off the windshield of the neighbor's car. It's November but the sun is still strong enough to throw some heat from time to time. Too bad those days are numbered.

I cross the street, duck under the bare branches of the old oak tree on the edge of the campus, and cut through UHolloway on my way to the Y. The empty basketball court on top of the bluff is begging me to come play, but if I stop, sooner or later the campus cops will come by and throw me off. They leave you alone in the summer when there's no school, but when the students are back, they move you along pretty quick.

It's a sweet place to hoop, like something you'd see in a movie. The court is on this high hill, so you can see the whole city and the river cutting right through the middle, but because it's surrounded by a high chain link fence, the ball doesn't roll away. It's got chain nets too, so when you make a shot it sounds like a cash register opening in a hurry—ka-ching!

We played some serious ball there this summer. Worked Boyd hard, getting him ready to play at that prep school of his. Had some serious Superman vs. Spider-Man ragers. Old School needed help, too, not that he'll ever admit it. If you want to impress the people who really know hoops, your game has to travel. You have to be able to play team ball and have some street in your game.

Besides the po-po, the only problem with the court is how close it is to the U's nuclear reactor. That's right, nu-cle-ar reactor. The school painted it white so it looks like a big marshmallow, because it's harmless, right? Most people just ignore it, but I watched *Chernobyl* with OT so I know there's some scary stuff sitting under that dome.

The last building on the block is the U's gym, a huge, top-heavy building that looks like it's about ready to keel over. All I can hear when I walk past is the loud sucking sound of its ventilation system. It's just like their basketball team—they haven't won anything in years.

Still, if I were my bro, the U would've been my fallback school. Fine, it's D3, a Massachusetts state college, but he could have stayed home, played here, dominated like you know he would have, then moved on to bigger and better things. A lot can happen in a year.

He didn't mind working here, filling orders at the food warehouse next to the reactor, keeping the cafeteria stocked. I used to go in for snacks. Anything in a damaged box was free game, and the quality of the available snacks got better later in the day as the forklift driving got worse. An ice-cold strawberry Nesquik from the walk-in cooler was my go-to all summer long.

The sun hits me again as its bounces back at me from the Y's glass doors. I slip inside and give my eyes a sec to adjust to the dark hallway. As they do, I hear the sweet sounds of Marla chatting with the ladies from yoga at the front desk. Her friendly voice is my ticket inside for some free hoops. It's not sneaking in if she lets me do it, right?

OT doesn't have the coin to get me a membership, so it's supposed to cost me $10 a day to play. That's why a lot of kids don't show on Sundays, when yoga has the gym in the morning and the court isn't free till the afternoon. You can play all day for the same price on Saturdays. That's when everyone shows. So Saturday is the day to play and Sunday is the day me and Wick work on our games.

I slip by the desk like a secret just to be safe. Marla isn't going to call me back—she won't embarrass me like that and I'm not going to make a big show of walking right by the desk without paying and embarrass her either. The other thing that speeds me up is trying to avoid the weird combination of perfume and sweat rising from the ladies. The two together remind me of NyQuil—trying to hide something nasty under something sweet never works.

Wick is inside the gym already, shooting hoops. He looks the same as usual, all arms and legs, with the same old classic do, tight on the sides and thick as a Brillo pad on top. But his game looks way different. He used to be all about action in the paint, but on my walk over, I haven't seen him take anything except jumpers from distance, and he hasn't missed one yet.

The only other people in the gym are an old man and a little kid. The guy, either the kid's dad or a trainer, is running him through some drills.

Post Malone's "White Iverson" echoes around the gym from Wick's Bluetooth speaker set up against the wall. I'll never understand why Malone did a song comparing himself to Iverson. It makes him sound like a loser—he doesn't want to practice, he doesn't want to pass, he doesn't want anything to do with his team. That's why he never won a championship. He didn't share the rock, so his teammates never developed. It's like Rodrigo. Next to me, he was probably the most talented kid at the Y, but his team finished in last place every season he played.

We had some tough losses on the Blazers, but at least we took care of business last season. I wish we could run it back. Everyone wants to level up this year...it's just too bad we have to do it in different places. Boyd and Old School at their prep school, and me and Wick at Holloway High. Then again, there probably aren't enough spots on the high school freshman team for all of us anyway.

"Yo, Romeo," Wicks says as I give him dap.

"What up, brah?" I answer. "Why you calling me Romeo?"

"Because I never know wherefore art thou," he says. "I've been here about fifteen minutes."

"Sorry, I been busy." I drop my duffel in the corner, take out my ball and my court shoes, and start to lace up.

I appreciate Wick grabbing one of the baskets with a glass backboard. The temporary baskets on the sides of the gym have no style whatsoever. They're low, uneven, and the rims don't have any give. The worst part is the dull thud the ball makes when you try to bank one in. The backboards sound like they're made from wood filler.

"Busy with what? It can't be school work. I've seen your grades."

"I'm all about the Bs this year," I shoot back. Once I say it out loud, I realize it doesn't sound that impressive. "Not everyone is a genius like you."

I stand up and start to get loose. My first few shots catch too much rim, and roll off to the left or the right. I have to go find my rebounds and it feels like I'm doing more walking than shooting.

"I'm no genius, I just put in the work," he says back. "More than I want to. You should see the way my pops rides me."

"Believe me, OT is all over me, too."

I finally sink a shot. It's about time. Weird thing is, never mind Wick not missing, I don't think I've seen him touch the rim yet.

"I'm just psyched my pops is gonna let me try out for hoops," he says, the whites of his eyes flashing against his dark skin. "I didn't see that coming. If Coach hadn't made the jump from the Y to Holloway High, I don't think he would have. I still had to ask Coach to talk to him, explain how playing ball will help round out my resume for colleges."

"So you think you've got it made?"

It sounds like he's on the inside track to making the team. Is Coach really gonna talk up the team to his dad then cut him? Doubt it. And there will be cuts. Lots of them. Something like a hundred kids are gonna be fighting for all of ten spots.

"No way. We're going to have to earn it. None of us is getting any special treatment. You know Coach don't play like that."

My next shot lands on the back of the rim, sits there a sec, then plops in. It's a make, but it's still ugly as all get out.

"My pops is so down for me playing, he's giving me time to work on my game. He got me a membership here and sent me to those shooting camps over the summer."

Those shooting camps? I knew Wick went home to visit his family in India but I didn't know anything about any camps. It looks like he got some quality instruction there. I've never been to a camp in my life—even in this country. And I spent my summer trying to help Boyd get better. The way Wick is drilling his jumpers, I'm starting to wonder if I should have done something different. What if he makes the team over me? That would be hard to live down.

"You want to play taps?" he asks.

He must be thinking the same thing as me, because it's like he wants to see how he measures up. I'd rather play one-on-one than some shooting game because I'm a streaky shooter, and if my outside shot isn't falling, I can't switch it up and try to score from somewhere else. But I'm not about to back down either.

"All day," I say.

"Going to twenty-one, right?"

"Always."

Taps is basically a game of free throws, and when you miss, your opponent can replace you at the line by getting your rebound and tipping it in before their feet come back to the ground. But if they miss, or don't get off the floor before getting to the ball, you stay.

The scoring works just like real basketball, with field goals worth two points and free throws worth one. If you don't get to 21 exactly, you go back to 11. So the best part is when you get to 19, because you have a decision to make. Are you sure you can make those last two pressure free throws? Or do you want to miss on purpose, wait for your opponent's next miss, and convert the easy field goal for the win?

He hands me his ball. "You start."

I put my Wilson back in my duffel. Balls sometimes walk away here, and I'm not taking any chances. It's easy to lose track when you're in the heat of a game. I had to beg OT for that ball, and if I lose it, the chances of me getting the kicks I want are going to be zero.

I go to the free throw line and miss my first shot. It rolls off the side of the rim and straight to Wick on the block. He leaps, catches it in midair, and redirects the ball off the backboard and though the hoop. He knocked me off the line just like that! His coordination always surprises me—you wouldn't think a kid with arms down to his knees would be able to move them like that.

"Like taking candy from a baby," he says.

I don't have a ready comeback, which isn't like me, but I didn't expect any trash talk outta him. Sounds like he learned more than just shooting at those camps.

We switch spots and he goes to the line while I wait on the block for him to miss. And wait. And wait.

He drains six free throws in a row. I catch a break when he finally misses and his rebound comes off the rim nice and easy. He lulled me to sleep with all his makes, but the soft rebound gives me time to recover. I jump late, so I have to go sideways to get to the ball, but I still manage to flip it one-handed off the backboard and into the basket before coming back to the ground. It's a move that would even impress Spider-Man!

"Baby's growing up fast," I say. It's kind of sad though, because I had to hold onto it for so long.

I'm down 8-2, so it's my turn to go on a run. I make six straight shots to tie it. Then I take a little extra time to make him think about how my next shot is going to break the tie and—of course—I miss. The shot barely hits the front rim and drops straight down. Good thing is, he doesn't have any time to get to the rebound before it hits the floor.

I take a deep breath and go back to my normal motion and make my next two. But you know I can't stand success, so I miss my third attempt and he converts the rebound.

He goes on another crazy run and hits his next nine shots. He shoots each one the same exact way, total confidence, and I'm really sweating now. This is starting to get embarrassing. At 19, he pauses, like he's trying to decide whether to miss his next one on purpose so he can win by tapping in my miss to get to 21.

"Don't put too much pressure on yourself," I say. "But if I get back to that line, I'm not getting off."

"I don't feel pressure," he says, resting his eyes on me a little too long, like he's trying to make a point. Then he goes into his shot and drains his next free throw to get to 20. When I get the rebound out of the net, I spin it back to him, hoping to throw him off a little. No dice. He drills the game-winner at 21.

"Ball don't lie," he says, then walks over to his bag and grabs a drink.

"Want to go again?" I ask without leaving the court. I don't feel like I deserve a drink after turning in that performance. Besides, all I have is water anyway, with Pax leaving his job at the food warehouse. "And this time, let's make it a little more challenging. You know how to play Threes?"

"Of course."

His technique from the free throw line has obviously gotten better, but threes come so far from the hoop it has to be a different story. Especially with those long-ass arms of his.

"Loser's ball," he says with a smirk and comes back to the court.

"Got that right," I answer.

I go directly under the basket and lay it in. Then I go to the free throw line and nail that. Next I run out to the three-point line and drain it. In threes, if you make your three, you stay outside and keep shooting them, but once you miss, you're out.

This is my game! It's more like one-on-one because you get to shoot from different places on the court. The variety helps me get on a roll. I just have to make sure I don't get bored and lose my focus. Of course, as soon as I start thinking, I do just that, and miss my second three.

Still, 6-0 isn't a bad start.

Now it's his turn. He makes his layup, then his free throw too, but he misses his three. Just like I thought.

"Still throwing up bricks from out there," I say. I'm up 6-3.

"I'll do better when I get the ball back," he says.

"If you get the ball back." I make my layup and free throw to get to nine. My hands finally feel warm and my grip is so tight I can actually feel the dimples on the ball. I drain four threes in a row to win the game at 21.

"I'm guessing you're up to rematch that," he says, shooting me a dark look.

He's normally super-friendly, all bright eyes and smiles. But when he gets mad, his eyes narrow and his smile disappears. We lose power at the condo all the time, and him getting mad feels kind of like that. Things turn black and it puts you on edge because you don't know what's gonna happen next.

"Let's go one-on-one," I say. I can't help myself.

"I thought we were just working on our games today."

"What? You afraid to go up against me?"

"Of course not," he says. "I just need a quick minute to catch my breath."

He walks over to his stuff, takes a deep swig, and leans back against the padding under the hoop. Just beyond him, the old man on the other end is all up in the kid's grill. He's not talking loud, but you can tell from his body language, and the way he's jabbing his arm into the kid's chest, that he's letting him hear it. He has to be his dad, because you couldn't treat someone you weren't close to like that.

"Brah, we can do better than this," Wick says to me as I walk over to my duffel for my own drink.

"What do you mean? I feel pretty good right now."

"What I mean is, we have to stop going at each other," he says. "We both have the same goal, right? Playing for Holloway High."

"Yeah, but the problem is, we're both trying out for the same team."

I go and stand next to him. "True, but it doesn't have to mean we're competing with each other. We've always been teammates. If we do this right, we'll still be teammates. Basketball is about skills, of course, but it's about chemistry, too. We have to show that in the tryouts—that we can raise our games by working together. You know, the sum is greater than the parts."

"I guess, but how do we do that?" His math reference might make sense to another genius, but he's gotta know the only IQ I have is a basketball IQ. "Tryouts is pretty much every man for himself."

"It doesn't have to be," he says. "Especially since we're going to start with open gyms."

Technically, tryouts don't start until December, because that's when basketball season officially begins. But open gyms are gonna start any day now, and you might as well call them tryouts. Coach isn't running things, but you know he'll be there. Watching everything.

"Think about it," Wick keeps going. "We have to get noticed, right? Coach knows us. But he's only the freshman coach. The varsity and JV coaches have a say, too. Maybe even more than him. We have to stand out to them, too."

"Well, the easiest way to get noticed is to hustle," I say. I know it, because Coach is always preaching that effort is the only thing you can really control. "But how do we make that a team effort?"

"By pushing each other."

I feel that. If there is one new thing I worked on this summer, it was my conditioning. For once, my butt is in running shape. Old School insisted we run together and I'm glad he did.

"OK, I got that."

"But here's the difference maker," he says. "When we scrimmage—and it's open gym so we're going to scrimmage a lot—we have to make sure each of us gets our touches, and gets them where we want the ball."

"Makes all the difference."

"Definitely. Most of the kids trying out will be playing an individual game, trying to showcase themselves. There won't be a lot of passing going on, which is really what you need to get a good look. With us working together, we'll get those good looks."

"I'm down," I say, nodding slowly as Post Malone goes to "Congratulations" and the notes at the beginning weave through the rafters above us. I feel a smile break across my face big enough to make Boyd proud.

Four

My dad's journal—and Pax's notes—run through my head as I sit in homeroom zoning out and waiting for the morning bell. This flimsy desk is nothing like Pax's, that's for sure. I almost brought the whole thing down when I slid into it.

I started reading at the very beginning and kept going until I had to leave to catch the bus:

Started school today. We have classes in Boston before we head to San Fran for staging.

Classes are really interesting. The things they tell you about ambushes and such! I get more and more scared every day. How does anyone survive a year over there?

2nd day of school. Sat thru classes. One guy is heading back for a second tour. He is real gung-ho and loves to push his weight around. When we were cleaning our weapons, he got a rag stuck in his M-4 and everyone jumped on him. Serves him right.

3rd day of school. Went to range to test our marksmanship. My blood pressure shot up, I bet. Saw old Johnny Lee. Amazing how fired up Johnny Lee is—what a change ha ha. Smitty and I gave him a hard time. Hope those guys end up all right. Got back from school late.

4th day of school. Felt good this morning. Chaplain came around. I went to church and received communion. What a change— funny what war does.

Last day of school. After class Smitty and I came back and drank some beers—might as well drink now because once we get to Afghanistan we won't dare.

Leaving next week. I will be glad to get to my unit. I have a job to do. Those people need our help and I am proud to be able to help them. I have to admit I'm a little scared, though. Hope all turns out well.

My bro added notes to the side of this one, too:

M-4—Assault rifle
Smitty, Johnny Lee—who are these guys? Where are they now?
Drinking beers? Really? Are we partying or going to war?
He also drew a line under the part where my dad wrote:
I have a job to do. These people need our help and I am proud to be able to help them.
Then he added:
So why didn't you get the job done?

I don't get why Pax is taking it so personal. Like it's my dad's fault they bombed the Mouse! He has a better feel for my dad than I do, obviously, but I never got the impression from anyone that he was a screwup. He died when I was only a few years old, so I don't have much to go on other than what the family and the press clippings say. Maybe it's all bull. Pax seems to think so.

I usually hang in front of the clock with everyone else before school, but I just wasn't up to it this morning. I was the first one in class, which is a first. I even beat Coach.

Mario pimp-walks through the door, followed by an entourage. Mario isn't his real name but it's what everyone calls him, because he looks like Super Mario from the old school video games. He's short and thick, with a wide nose and dark curly hair.

A couple girls are following him. I don't bother to turn my head to take a tally, but out of the corner of my eye I try to find out if Lea is in the mix. I'm glad to see she's not.

Wick comes down my aisle and leans in to talk to me. The top of my desk creaks louder than his whisper. "You hear anything about his tickets?"

I shake my head no.

He nods toward Mario, like he wants us to go talk to him. I shake my head no even harder. There's no way we're gonna walk over there and add to the list of people kissing his butt.

The kid is super-popular these days, and it's not because of his effervescent personality either. His dad has some kind of connection and he gets tickets to the biggest Celtics games. The Lakers are coming to town on Veterans' Day, and because the two teams are in opposite conferences, they only play once a year, unless they meet in the finals, of course. The Lakers and the Celtics are the winningest teams in NBA history, but whenever they match up in the playoffs these days, LeBron sends the C's home. So yeah, it's kind of a big deal.

Mario actually had the stones to send a sign-up sheet around the class for us to add our names to if we're interested in going. As if he doesn't already know everyone wants to go. I do, obviously, the C's are my boys. I've only been to one game, which was actually an open practice they held at the U a couple years back, where they didn't even scrimmage. Still, I just couldn't bring myself to throw my name down. I just passed the paper on to Rodrigo in front of me.

Lea glides down the aisle after Wick goes back to his desk. She has perfect posture and holds herself as straight as a model balancing a book on her head. Even though she's tall, she has kind of a big butt, which I'm guessing is really muscle, because the girl can run like the wind. When she runs, her long black hair flows behind her like a kite with streamers. I know because that's the view I had when we raced in PE at the start of the year. She crushed it, and no one came close to touching her, not even me and my newfound legs.

Coach walks in last and does a double take when he sees me in my seat already. I'm the one who should be doing a double take. He's been my teacher for over a month, but seeing him in a shirt and tie instead of a T-shirt still weirds me out.

I've got to give him credit, though, because his class moves right along. Most of the time anyway. You can tell he takes teaching as seriously as basketball because he says he only speaks when it's important and he probably talks more in class than he does in practice. He's all in too—I heard he's even teaching night school.

It's funny though, because he still has a gym rat vibe—especially on a morning like this, when his pinhead is looking a little shiny. I bet he played old-man basketball before school and his shower didn't take. Me and Wick went to the Y early one Monday when there was no school— Columbus Day or something—and we saw him leaving the court with a bunch of other geezers. He protects himself with all kinds of armor—arm sleeves with padded elbows and double knee braces. We could hear his braces squeaking all the way down the hallway. Is hanging with your boys worth all of that?

"Good morning, everyone," Coach says, and takes his seat at the front.

"Morning, Mr. Moore," a couple kids say nonchalantly, while most ignore him. It's nothing like the response he demands from his players. I'm waiting for him to ask for more when Principal Perkins breaks in over the tinny intercom and starts squawking out the announcements.

It's the usual PTO bake sale, progress report type of stuff, so I go back to zoning out, until I notice Wick's Brillo pad turn my way from across the room. I perk up and hear Perkins say something about the start of open gym for basketball. Tomorrow night! I'll be ready.

Next, Perkins asks us to stand for the pledge of allegiance and starts squawking that out. Most of us stand, but a few kids sit it out. OT was outraged when he heard the pledge was going to be optional this year. He made sure I understood I was going to stand straight and tall out of respect for my dad and he better not hear any different.

Rodrigo stands up in front of me and starts rocking his fuzzy head back and forth like the top of OT's old pressure cooker. It gets my attention right away because he usually sits for the pledge. Then I take a longer look and I can tell he's moving his head in time with Carmen, who sits to his side, almost like they're listening to the same song through different earbuds.

I step closer to Rodrigo to see what's up and it turns out he's mocking her. Carmen is Dominican and her English isn't that great. She tries really hard but she overdoes it—moving her head real dramatically, opening her mouth bigger than she should, lolling her tongue about and everything.

Rodrigo is doing all of that—only he exaggerates it even more. My ears start to tingle as I look to the front to check on Coach. He's standing by his desk and facing the flag in the corner, with absolutely no idea of what's going on.

I take a few steps forward until I'm dead even with Rodrigo. His face opens up in a maniacal smile, the scraggly hairs in the middle of his unibrow jutting out in every direction. He thinks I moved up to get a better view, like I'm in on the joke, which makes me even madder. I give him a death stare but he just keeps on going.

It's more than I can take so I raise the elbow of the arm over my heart a little higher, then brush him back with it, kind of like I would in a basketball game when I've got the ball and I need to clear some space to protect it.

Rodrigo acts just like he would on a basketball court, too—he flops! I didn't hit him anywhere near hard but he falls back toward his desk anyway, flailing with his arms over his head, working it like he's trying to get me thrown out of the game.

His timing is perfect because he hits his desk just as everyone finishes the pledge. He lands on top of it with a loud thud and the legs squeak as the desk skids backward along the floor.

Everyone stops and stares, and the only thing I can hear any more is the buzzing in my ears. I look to the front of the class again and this time Coach is staring me right in the eyes.

"Noel! Rodrigo! In the hallway! Now!"

Rodrigo gives me side-eye as we follow Coach out. I don't even bother to acknowledge him.

"Noel?" Coach turns to face me and stops talking, as if that's all he has to say. Because it is. He likes to act all nonchalant, but at the same time, he hates it when you don't take him seriously, so when you screw something up, he makes sure you feel the pain.

Rodrigo answers for me: "He didn't like the way I was saying the pledge. Too much enthusiasm."

"Enthusiasm, huh?" Coach asks. "That's interesting. You usually can't be bothered to get out of your seat."

I can't keep my mouth shut any longer. "You're full of it. You were messing with Carmen." I probably wouldn't have said anything if I wasn't so fired up, but it's not ratting him out if I say it to his face, right?

Coach just exhales and puts a hand on my shoulder to make sure I stay put.

He looks over at Rodrigo. "From now on, say the pledge like a normal person, or sit it out."

"Got it," he says.

"OK. You're all set."

Rodrigo winks at me and heads back to class. I try to go, too, but Coach tightens his grip on my shoulder.

"So, what was that about?" he asks.

"I just said it—he was mocking Carmen." Isn't it obvious?

"If it's something more, let me know." He leans in as he says it, like he's trying to read my mind. "I know you have a lot going on right now."

"Like what exactly?"

"Well, the president has been tweeting some pretty troubling stuff."

The buzzing in my ears has now moved to my head. Hopefully it's going to block him from reading my thoughts. Because getting into all of this with him is about the last thing I want to do.

"Coach, you gotta know I'm not into politics."

"Politics can get personal pretty quick," he says. Maybe he actually can read my mind, because why would he keep going otherwise? "Your dad was a vet, right? And Pax has to be eighteen by now. I have to say, I didn't know those tweets were going to take such a dark turn when we started this unit."

"It don't bother me one bit. We almost done here? The class is gonna think you're making this thing with Rodrigo into a much bigger deal than it is."

"Almost. I know tryouts are around the corner. You thinking you and Rodrigo might end up battling for a spot?"

"I'm going to be battling a lot of kids for a spot. I'm not going to take the competition out one at a time—I plan to let my game do that."

"OK, great," he says, finally letting go of my shoulder. "Just had to ask, I guess."

I try to reassure him by ending on a positive note. "Besides, there's always the Y."

Too bad there's no escape from the drama. "Noel, that's not the place for you. Continuing to dominate there will only hold you back. You need to take it to the next level. You have a good shot to make the high school team. Just make sure you show everyone your best self. Don't get caught up in any petty stuff."

So it's Holloway High or nothing? The throbbing in my head has faded to a dull ache. Which feels like it's going to stay with me for a while.

"Coach, I got a killer headache, can I see the nurse for an Advil or something?"

"Sure," he says, and heads back into the classroom. "I'll write you a note."

I follow him back to his desk and wait for him to scribble out a pass. Everyone just stares at me. I made it even easier for them by not going right back to my desk to hide. I don't scan the room or anything, because I don't want to know Lea's reaction, but I can tell by the looks on the faces I do see, that while Rodrigo may have been acting like a total jerk, they think I'm the real jackass.

Five

From the next section of my dad's journal:

Jenny helped me pack this morning. She ironed all my clothes. No need for that—I think she was just trying to keep herself busy. Mother and Father came over to say goodbye. Had to leave quickly, almost in tears. My folks minded Pascal as Jenny drove me to Logan. She cried and cried.

As the plane took off, I watched Boston disappear in the night. All I could see in my mind was Jenny in tears. I'm starting to have second thoughts. Am I really doing the right thing here? Leaving my wife and little one behind?

Arrived in San Fran and got a room. Got up and went to Oakland. Saw all my old friends from training—filled out forms, got clothing issue, and such.

Got up and made formation. Smitty (friend from AIT) and I fell out to give blood. Gave blood, almost fainted—tired and rundown I guess—goofed off rest of day.

My name was finally called. When they called my name, it felt strange—a funny feeling came over me—at last I am on my way. I called Jenny. It is hardest on her. I will be glad when I finally get there and all this sloppiness is over!

5 a.m. comes—board plane and leave U.S. behind. I hope I make it back.

After flying for over 20 hours, I am finally here!

They put us on a Chinook and send us to FOB Jalalabad. What a ride. It's night and even though we are protected by two gunners, I'm expecting to be fired on at any moment.

I learn I am assigned to the Korengal Outpost. I'm a little concerned from what I've heard. The guys said there's only one road in and out and the Taliban have eyes on you at all times. You have to drive real slow to look out for IEDs along the road—which just makes you a sitting duck for RPGs and snipers.

BZZZZT! BZZZZT!

My phone is vibrating on the window sill next to me like an angry bee trying to find a way out. I don't want to take the call—reading this stuff is hard enough without interruptions. But I need to stop the buzzing before it brings my headache back.

I lean over the desk to check the caller ID and see it's my Aunt Mary. I pick it up, but before answering, I give my bro's notes a quick scan:

AIT—Advanced Individual Training
Chinook—Military helicopter
FOB—Forward Operating Base
Taliban—Bad guys
Korengal Outpost (aka KOP)—Bad news! The Taliban was strong in the valley to begin with, and when we replaced the local lumber mill with our fort, we put it out of business. Most of the guys who lost their jobs joined the bad guys.

"Noel! That you?"

The loudmouth in my ear isn't my aunt. It's my Uncle Jack, which isn't good news, because I'm going to have to talk to him, then talk to my aunt, too. I stash the journal again before OT gets home and catches me with it.

"Uh, yeah. I'm here."

"Great! I'm glad you picked up. So, what are you thinking about all this draft talk?" What, is Uncle Jack on Twitter, too? He seems kind of old for it. Although the president's tweets have to be all over the news by now. "Just saying, you might want to think about enlisting. This could be a big moment for you!"

"I'm only fifteen. I don't think the president is that desperate."

"Oh man, that's right, I'm sorry. Pax is the one who's eighteen. You guys are the same size so I get confused." I'm about the same height as my bro, which is especially convenient now that he's gone because I can dip into his closet for shirts and shoes...but still. He's got a full beard and the next time I have to shave will be my first. "Is he around?"

"No. He's in Florida."

"No way! That's a brave kid, heading out after all that stuff went down. Smart too. I bet he got a real cheap flight. He's exactly the kind of guy we need to finish the job!"

"Yeah, I guess."

I'm surprised how fired up he is. Maybe the president should put him in charge of recruiting. With Uncle Jack leading the way, he might not need that draft after all.

"Man, if I was eighteen. I'd sign up this instant. Never mind waiting for the draft. Just go and do it. Pax's a lucky man. This is his chance to go out and do something big! Something he'll remember the rest of his life!"

I want to ask why he didn't ever go out and do something big—because if he did, I don't remember hearing about it.

"Jack, stop harassing him!"

I can hear my aunt in the background and it sounds like she's trying to get to the phone. It might take a while—Jack's about twice her size. If he blocks her out, I doubt her little arms will be long enough to get around his wide body.

"Sorry about that, Noel," my Aunt Mary has the phone now. She's breathing so heavy I don't think my uncle made it easy for her. "I don't know what that was all about. Imagine a fifteen-year-old joining the Army!"

"It's all good," I say. "He thought he was talking to Pax."

"So Pax went down there, huh? I'm a little surprised my dad let him go."

"Technically speaking, Pax is an adult now." I'm not exactly sure when you become a man, but if you can get drafted and sent to war, you're there already.

"Of course," she says. "Anyway, how are things with you?"

"Good."

"I tried the house phone first but no one answered. That's when Jack got the bright idea to call your cell."

"Oops, sorry about that." I had no idea the phone was ringing downstairs. I head down to check that I didn't miss any others. OT won't be happy if he called to check on me and I didn't pick up. "I was just really into my...homework."

"You won't hear me complain about that!" she says with a laugh. "So how is your grandfather? Up to speed with his meds?"

"As far as I know."

"OK, just try to keep tabs on him. He misses a dose from time to time."

"I know."

"The two of you are good kids, but raising two teenage boys is still a lot of work. He raised your father and me, of course, but he's that much older now. And he can't forget to take care of himself."

"I'm on it." I don't understand why I'm supposed to double-check his dispenser...it's not like he's blind or something. But it's fine.

"So all's good with you?"

"Yeah, of course. Why wouldn't I be OK?"

Why does everyone keep hitting me with what's basically the same question—am I OK? Aren't my answers good enough?

"Please, don't get upset. Isn't everyone on edge right now? It's not unreasonable to think you might be anxious about things. They raised the terror alert to the highest it's been in years and the president's talking up his war every chance he gets."

I check the downstairs phone and a wave of relief washes over me when I see I only missed that one call from my aunt. I'm trying to think up an excuse to get off the phone and get back to the journal when I realize my aunt might be able to save me some time.

"Auntie, can I ask you something?"

"Of course. What is it?"

"All this stuff going on has me thinking about my dad. I don't remember him saying too much about Afghanistan. Did he ever talk to you about it?"

"Not really. He didn't like to talk about it much...at least not with his little sister anyway."

The way she answers slowly, like she's picking at her words, it doesn't sound like she likes to talk about it much either. But what do I care? She didn't mind playing twenty questions with me earlier, whether or not I liked it. I sit at the kitchen table as I give her a turn on the hot seat.

"So he never talked about it?"

"Not so much. You could tell it bothered him a bit. So I don't think he'd want you or Pax to be rushing off and getting yourselves into anything. I'm glad Pax decided to take that break. He'd be better off at school, but at least he's not sitting home doing nothing. I'm sure he's doing something productive—hopefully looking at more colleges or something like that."

Yeah, I'm sure he's up to something productive all right—that's what I'm worried about.

"Anyway, you especially must remember how your dad felt about guns."

"Oh yeah," I nod. "How could I forget?"

OT wouldn't let me play with toy guns when I was a kid out of respect for my dad's wishes. I hated that. I couldn't even play cops and robbers with the neighborhood kids. I mean I tried, but what could I do without a gun? It was a joke, me running around with a bent stick for a weapon, one I had to hide whenever I was anywhere near the house.

"You said it bothered him a bit. What else did you notice?"

"Well, I don't know. Sometimes he'd get sad around the holidays, kind of quiet. He said he felt guilty about the impact the war had on families. On both sides of the war.

"Don't get me wrong," she adds quickly. "I'm not saying he was always like that. Or that he wasn't proud to serve. He joined the reserves after 9/11, but he didn't get called up until years and years later. The war seemed like it had been going on forever by that point.

"Anyway, sometimes he'd get in a mood and would turn pretty quiet. He probably had PTSD, but we didn't know much about it then. I guess everyone just dealt with it the best they could. His way was to be alone. He'd go down to the den to watch classic basketball games or head out for a long drive."

The thought of one of those long drives just about kills the conversation. My dad liked to take the long way up to New Hampshire for tax-free beer and cigarettes, but he never came back from one of those trips.

Some guy who started the day at the bar ended it by taking his truck—snowplow and all—through a stop sign and my dad, too. Imagine surviving a year in Afghanistan then getting smashed by a drunk after you got back to the good old U.S.A.!

I googled it one day and saw the pictures that ran in the paper. My dad's little silver car crumpled like an empty beer can. No one needed an IED that day.

But I'm not going to get hung up on any orphan drama now. Peter Parker didn't have parents either and things worked out OK for him. I'm all about the present. I have to figure out what's going on with my bro, and the more I know about the journal, the better. I jump right back into my questions. One in particular has been burning in my brain for a while and now seems like the time to ask it.

"So, did he kill anybody?"

"I don't know, Noel...have you asked your grandfather about this?"

"No."

"You should. He'll know more than me."

I think I should too, but there's a problem with that. If I do, I'll have to tell him about Pax, what he's writing about my dad, what he might be thinking about doing himself, and I don't want to raise OT's blood pressure any higher than it already is.

"I will."

"Good. All I know is, he was in a lot of firefights. He said they'd just be shooting into whatever the cover was, aiming at rifle flashes, firing and ducking, but according to him anyway, he never really saw what came of it."

I've got one last question, but I'm not sure how to ask. So I decide to finesse it. "Coach—my English teacher—told us a lot of veterans wrote diaries, to help them process what they went through..."

"And you want to know if your dad...wrote one?" She is picking her words more carefully than ever, like she's trying to avoid stepping through a mess. "Well, I think he did...your mother might have said something about it...it was a long time ago."

"So he did write something—did you read it?"

"I didn't...I didn't say that. Sorry Noel, I've got to get dinner ready. Jack likes an early supper. Tell my dad I was asking about him."

"Yeah, sure, see you."

I put my phone down, harder than I should, and it slaps against the table. So which is it? Did my aunt read the journal or not? What is it, some kind of weird family secret?

Too bad the people who seem to know the most about it aren't here to answer my questions. My dad's six feet under, my mom is God-knows-where, and my bro's a thousand miles away. I'm not about to add any more to OT's plate either—he's gone way beyond the call of duty already.

Six

The bright headlights of the minivan cut right through my head trip about my dad as Wick's mom pulls up to my spot on the steps. I read about some real action today:

Got up around midnight and packed my stuff and waited for transport to the outpost. We're all a bit nervous—I hope all turns out well. Got in a couple Chinooks and flew out.

After another night ride we arrived at Korengal. I met the captain—seems like a real nice guy—friendly and interested. I like him. Met my platoon. Tim is our squad leader. Members are Larry, Dutch, Lee, and Murphy. They seem like a bunch of nice guys. They were very friendly and made me feel at home. I am glad I have finally reached my unit. These guys seem all right.

We did some walking in the afternoon, came back around 5 and had MREs for dinner. Guys let me have the beefsteak in honor of my first real day. To be honest I actually enjoyed it.

We went on an armored patrol with the Humvees. It was real interesting but I was never so scared in my life. The company searched a road out of the valley—what they call a road around here anyway. More like a trail. It ran through the middle of a green valley with fields and thick forests. I guess I thought it would be barren out here, all desert or something. There sure are plenty of mountains. Very steep terrain. And lots of places for bad guys to hide. We found a weapons cache in a cave—rifles, RPGs, mortars, other random stuff.

Patrolled with another unit. They went in first and made contact. We went in right behind them. M-4 worked good—just jammed up once. Found unexploded IEDs and such after the fight. I was kind of scared and sweaty and nauseous—sweat just about poured off me.

On the way back, we were point. Hit an IED and the impact blew off the front wheels. Somehow no one was hurt bad. All real shook up though. The guys say we got lucky. IED must have been poorly made. It was weird unique experience—scared me a lot.

Afterward Murphy got overly emotional and started yelling at the people along the road. No call for that. I grabbed him and shut him up.

Found out Tim caught shrapnel right next to me. He is all right though. Leaves for R&R tomorrow.

After his usual acronym busting, Pax added the most positive commentary I've seen so far:

MRE—Meal Ready to Eat
R&R—Rest and Recuperation
Close calls but finally got something done!
Way to get Murphy's back!
Let's GO!

I get up from my crouch and go to the car. Wick's my ride to open gym and it's time to execute on our plan.

We'll show up together and stay as close as we can the rest of the night. Everyone else will play an iso game on both ends—selfish on offense and overaggressive on defense—and we're gonna work together to take advantage of the whole thing.

The noise from the courts hits us as soon as we walk into the main entrance of the school. It's the usual playlist: sneakers squeaking off the floor, balls pounding the court and backboards, rims rattling after missed shots. The one thing missing is chatter—so you know everyone is already all wrapped up in their own little world.

The Holloway High gym has the same six-hoop setup as the Y but it feels a lot smaller. Besides the dozens of kids packed in here, it's really dark, too. The school's primary color is red and the walls are painted a shade of red so deep it's almost purple. A section of stands is folded back against the far wall and that's red, too. It's a tough shooting backdrop. All the red runs straight through the glass backboards and makes it hard to find the rims.

I scan the sea of kids for the coaching staff, but I don't see any of them. It's not officially basketball season yet, so they can't run this anyway, but someone is going to have to do it. All of a sudden Boomer, the janitor, hustles to center court and pierces the air with his whistle: EEK! EEK! EEK!

Next he bellows instructions that can be heard in all corners of the gym. It's obvious how he earned his nickname and why he got picked to run this—he's basically a walking megaphone.

He wants us to run suicides. As he talks through it, a bunch of seniors step up and start to organize us into groups, setting us up in rows along the baseline. Wick shadows my every move and we end up in the second group of kids.

Boomer is giving instructions the whole time: "Run full-out from the baseline to the free throw line and back," he shouts. "Then to the half-court line and back, then to the opposite free throw line and back, then the full length of the court, and finally all the way back."

He pauses to catch his breath. Never mind running the drill, just describing it leaves him winded. Just because he works in a gym doesn't mean he works out.

He finally points to the first group of kids and blows his whistle again. As they take off, the coaches finally walk in—Coach Maguire, Coach Brady, who runs the JV, and my coach—Coach Moore.

As Wick and I step up with our group, I realize I'm already breathing hard. I haven't done anything yet, so it's just nerves. Which is fine, because I know nerves are as good a source of energy as any. I take a few deep breaths but try to keep it casual so no one notices.

The first group of kids to go don't get it—they aren't running all out. They think the suicides are just a warm-up, something to kill some time and burn some energy so we'll pay more attention to the next set of instructions, when the real drills start.

They're dead wrong. The coaches showed up in time to see this and they'll be watching it just as closely as they will everything else. They have to scout out a lot of kids, many they've never seen before, so they have to figure us out quick. And this drill is perfect for that. It's not about talent. It's about desire. It shows who wants to play in the worst way and who thinks they're too cool to go all out.

Our group gets ready to go next. We line up along the baseline, ready for the whistle, as the stragglers from the first group clear the court. Boomer whistles again and me and Wick are off flying.

We jump out of the box and to the front right away and pump our arms and legs hard to make sure we stay there. When we hit the free throw line and make the first turn back, we're already way ahead. We keep pushing hard and stay shoulder to shoulder all the way into the final turn. I get a step on him when we spin around, but I know he's right with me, because I can hear his quick, short breaths beside me. I ignore the burning in my lungs and do my best to keep my technique together so I can finish strong. I take first, then turn to slap Wick's hand as he comes in right behind me. We killed it.

We walk to the side to catch our breath as the next group takes off. The kids seemed to learn from the example we set. Instead of going through the motions like the first group, most of them are pushing it, too.

I sneak a peek over at the coaches as the kids make their first turn. Nobody is timing us or anything, but everyone is definitely paying close attention. The coaches are just looking for hustle here and the eye test is all you need for that.

After everyone runs, the seniors turn our groups into teams of five. The senior who is going to coach us, a tall, lanky kid named Steve, gives me and Wick a funny look, like he's onto us and might split us up. Then he smiles and motions for us to stay—it seems like he wants to win this thing and us working together can only help. We play it cool, but the way Wick relaxes his shoulders tells me he's as relieved as I am.

The seniors drop a mesh divider at center court, dividing the long gym into two smaller courts. We'll use the backup baskets at the sides of the court so they can run two games at once. You can see through the netting between the courts, but still, it's bad news because it means the coaches aren't going to see everything.

Our opponents are going to bring the ball down so we get set up on D. Me and Wick claim spots as the guards at the top of a 2-3 zone. We're probably not going to play guards this season, but it's the best place for us to get noticed. We're in position to shut down the other team's offense at the initial point of attack and we plan to do exactly that. The other kids on our side fill the spots behind us and we're ready to go.

Rodrigo, of all people, gets the inbound pass. He rubs the ball with his hands like a pitcher in baseball then starts dribbling down to face us. Wick shoots me a quick look and I know exactly what he's thinking. Rodrigo is going to walk right into our trap. The first thing he'll want to do is go to the basket, so we spread out so it looks like he has a lane to get there. His eyes light up like it's Christmas morning. They don't call me Noel for nothing!

He tries to drive right between us, and we both collapse on him when he does, extending our arms and smothering him. He has nowhere to go but he tries to dribble through us anyway. I poke the ball away, and Rodrigo doesn't even go for it, looking instead for the coach of his team to bail him out and call a foul. When I see him turn his head, I sprint toward our basket. Wick gets to the ball like I knew he would and throws it out ahead of me. I catch it in stride and kiss it off the backboard and in for the easy deuce.

The next time down, Rodrigo keeps his dribble but fakes a pass to the wing, apparently hoping to buy himself another half second to get past us, and charges right down the middle again. We jump in front to cut him off, and as he pulls back to avoid the foul, Wick rips the ball from his hands. Rodrigo is all over him, trying to get the ball back, but Wick manages to find space to make a bounce pass to me, then heads to the hoop himself. It's his turn for a bucket. And mine for an assist.

This time we won't score as easy, because we have a defender to contend with. One of Rodrigo's teammates has already lost confidence in him and stayed back in case he turned the ball over again. So I trail the play in case Wick needs another option. Wick goes to the hole, but the kid contests the layup, and he shoots it too strong. I see the whole thing develop and put myself in the perfect position to get the rebound, like we're playing taps. I leap, gather the rebound, and put it back up and in, all before I come back to the ground.

Rodrigo's not done yet. Next time down he jukes toward us, then steps back and takes a jumper. But his eyes betray him. I saw him peek up at the basket before he pretended to drive, measuring his shot, so I knew he was gonna let it fly.

I stay with him and jump in time to block the shot. I knock it back over his head and my momentum carries me right to it. It looks like I've got another bunny coming.

The same kid is hedging back on defense again, which is probably better than an open layup, because it'll give me a chance to dip into my bag of moves. Then I realize Wick hasn't scored yet. So I dribble at the defender, then gather myself like I'm going to elevate over him. But instead of taking the shot, I bounce a pass between my legs and behind me.

It's totally unnecessary and kind of a showboat move, but sometimes I just can't help it. Lucky for me, Wick guessed what I was about to do, and he's ready. What might have become a stupid turnover becomes the pretty assist I hoped it would be. The kid playing defense didn't even know anyone was behind me, so Wick sidesteps him easily and lays the ball up and in.

The seniors call a time-out and run subs. The kid coaching us is all high fives and smiles, like he saw it coming. We take a breather on the bench together and watch as the game proceeds without us. I'm dying to know how much Maguire saw, but there's no way I'm looking over to check. I don't want him to think I'm doing anything special here. This is just how I roll.

When we get back in the game, Rodrigo stays as far away from us as he can get, and another kid handles the ball. We don't get any more turnovers, so it's time to work on our half-court offense.

Wick takes the point, and I play the off-guard. I set up outside the elbow on the right side of the court, because I know that's where Wick wants to go. He runs toward me, I set a screen for him, and then I pop out to replace him at the top of the key. The defense overplays the pick and they both follow Wick. I'm left wide open. He kicks it back to me and I drain the three.

We run the same thing the next time down. I pick off Wick's defender, but mine stays with me this time, so Wick dribbles past me and right to the basket. Their big man comes over to protect it, but Wick fakes him out with an up and under move, then kisses it off the glass and in.

Rodrigo has had enough, and he picks me up on defense on our next possession. He blows up the pick and roll by jumping out at Wick then coming back to me. Wick knows the right play is to swing the ball to the other wing and not force anything, so that's what he does. The last thing we want to do is force a bad pass and give away a possession. You don't want coaches to think you're a turnover machine.

Still, the whole thing bothers me, because we set Rodrigo up to look good. Especially when the kid who gets the pass goes right into his shot, way too soon. Rodrigo is still enjoying the fact that he shut us down and he doesn't even think about boxing me out. So I hustle past him to get into rebounding position in case the kid misses. He obliges and I flip it back up and in.

The results aren't as dramatic the rest of the way. We know we can't just pass to each other all night, so we try to get the other kids involved. The defense focuses on us, which lets the other kids get open, and we're dropping dimes till they close the place.

Me and Wick leave the court together at the end of the night. I can feel the sweat cooling over just about every inch of my body so I know I worked hard. I feel good about that. I got my work in and I earned some respect.

When we hit the door, Coach Maguire is right there in the hallway, leaning against the back wall, and looking our way. I get the feeling he's been waiting for us.

He's a big guy, bigger than Coach even, like 6' 6" with a big frame, but there's nothing intimidating about him at all. He's gone soft—it's definitely been a long time since he's been in basketball shape. He's also got a big, baby face. He must shave multiple times a day because he doesn't have a trace of facial hair. Instead, he has these bright red cheeks, like his mommy just gave him a bath and scrubbed his face really hard.

Maybe his appearance explains why none of the colleges Pax was interested in would give him the time of day. They didn't take his baby-man coach seriously!

"Good job today, boys," he says. "You two make quite the tandem. I know you played a few seasons together at the Y. You guys do everything together?"

"No," we answer at the same time, which kind of defeats the point. I add a quick "Of course not," but it comes a little too late to help us.

"I figured," he says, adding a smile that forces dimples onto his cheeks. "So I'm really looking forward to the next open gym, where we'll set things up to get a better look at you as individuals."

Seven

OT is blasting the news on the living room TV, watching a guy with helmet hair and blinding teeth run through the latest from the president:

The president doubled down today on his demand for a draft to combat a renewed threat of terrorism in the wake of the October Surprise attacks.

He blamed the opposition for the need. As he tweeted early this morning: "We're out to make history, but let's be clear! We only need a draft because of the way Congress has gutted the military!"

Congressional leaders disagree on both the need for the war and the draft. They say it is premature to pick a perpetrator before the investigation into the attacks is complete. At this point, both foreign and domestic terror groups are considered suspect.

All sides agree, however, on the historic nature of the president's request. The last time the government called a draft was during the Vietnam War nearly 50 years ago.

The death toll for the coordinated attacks on the Magicland parks in California and Florida has now passed 1,000. It's still far from the infamous 9/11 attacks in 2001. About 3,000 people died that day, and health experts say roughly the same number died in the following few years as a result of exposure to toxic chemicals in the aftermath.

However, other potential impacts include the U.S. economy and the future of U.S. brands in international markets. The 9/11 attacks sent the U.S. economy into a tailspin and experts fear something similar in the wake of those in October. All Magicland parks worldwide remain closed—the U.S. ones for disaster recovery and the international ones for fear of additional attacks.

Meanwhile, marches against the president's call for war continue in major cities across the country...

"That's it for me," I say as I get up from the couch. "It's homework time."

"I'm glad you're taking school so serious this year," he says from behind a mouthful of his TV dinner. "Good thing that coach of yours became an English teacher, huh?"

"Yeah, sure," I call back, dropping my half-finished tray in the garbage and heading up the stairs. I wish I meant it. I never paid attention to current events until we started studying communications in Coach's class. Thing is, there's only so much of it I can take. I don't know how OT can stand watching the news on TV for hours every night. It's all bad news, with breaks in-between for ads from drug companies, whose products sound like they have more side effects than benefits.

Too bad the sound follows me up the stairs, even after I go to my room and shut the door. I have to turn my own TV on to drown it out. The Celtics pregame show is starting, so I go to lounge on my bed to watch, but not before taking the cover from the floor and throwing it on top. I don't know why, but an unmade bed doesn't bother me until I want to use it as something other than a bed. Of course, OT doesn't feel the same way. I'm supposed to make it when I'm done with it, not when I'm about to use it.

When I see we're playing the Knicks tonight, I feel like turning it back off. Don't get it twisted...I'm a huge fan, but the C's have gotten off to a bad start this season, and it'll be hard to get any satisfaction out of a game like this. The Knicks are so bad, you really can't win when you play them. If the C's win, it's no big deal, because they should have won easy, and if they lose, it's miserable to watch, because, again, they should have won. I decide to leave it on anyway—it's still better than what I'm hearing from the TV downstairs.

The news and the C's aren't the only reasons I'm in a bad mood. I couldn't find any time to read the journal all day. I want to pick up the pace but it's hard—I can't exactly get caught reading it with the way it's some kind of weird family secret.

I haven't heard from Pax in a while, so I send him a quick text: *Hey big bro, what up?*

I watch the message for a while but it just sits there, never even changing to delivered. Pax either turned off his phone or he's gone totally off the grid. I'm not sure what it means, but I don't feel good about it.

I've got no one but Google to answer my questions. Thanks to Coach's class, at least I know how to tell a good source from a bad one. OT says I spend most of the day staring at my phone anyway, so him seeing me on my phone isn't going to make him suspicious. I'll leave the TV on for more cover.

First, I check on Pax. I do a quick search to see if he's gone and done something big I haven't heard about yet. There are a few hits, but it's all Holloway High basketball stuff. Nothing new there.

Next, I try my dad. When I google his name, Rick Prince, the first thing that comes up is the story that ran in the paper after he died. They've got a picture of him in uniform, wearing desert camouflage, in front of an American flag, facing the camera but not smiling. He's got a square jaw, a shaved head, and a real serious look about him.

I skim the article because I already know the story. It calls him a local hero and lists his four medals—the National Defense Medal, Afghanistan Service Medal, Purple Heart, and Bronze Star. But it doesn't say how he got any of them.

I look the medals up and Wikipedia has the whole rundown—one is for serving in wartime, another is for serving in actual combat, the third is for getting wounded in combat, and the final one is for heroism. That last one, the Bronze Star, is supposed to be a big deal. But the obituary doesn't say what he did to earn it.

The story also talks about how he died. I can't say I remember an awful lot about the whole thing, but I do have one clear memory from the wake. I'm not sure why I did it—I guess I couldn't believe he was really dead—but I reached into the casket and touched his hand. It felt as cool as a brick in the shade. I knew it wasn't my dad in that casket. He was gone.

The volume on my TV changes and I look up to see the game is well underway. The Celtics are headed back to their huddle for a timeout, taking a ten-point deficit with them, and the Knicks fans are loving it. I have to shake my head. They're still not taking care of business.

I go back to my phone and google the war on terror. I don't even bother to read the hits I get there, because I can tell from the descriptions they're just a rehash of the news. The Magicland attacks, the draft, all of it. Same old, same old.

So I get more specific and search on the Korengal Outpost. There are plenty of hits on that. I start by browsing through the images to get a feel for the place. It's like my dad said. Steep mountains, rocky hillsides, uneven roads—everything looks tilted.

Some of the pics are action shots from the war, where the soldiers look like they're just firing into the air. There's no enemy to be seen anywhere. The soldiers are on the side of a mountain or behind a wall and it looks like they're firing at an invisible enemy. I guess that's what it felt like, too.

I visit the sites that have the best pics and go through their stories. Korengal was an Army base in the eastern part of the country near the border with Pakistan. None of the posts are that recent and I soon learn why. The Army closed the fort way back in 2010.

The soldiers called the place Death Valley because so many guys died there. It was built out in the open and you could only reach it by a single, narrow road like my dad said. No wonder he felt like a sitting duck.

The Taliban wanted to keep the fort on edge because it was set up close to their smuggling routes to their actual home country, Pakistan. They moved men, food, weapons, whatever they needed, through the valley, the same way they had been doing it for centuries, on foot or horseback. Pakistan was supposed to be an ally of ours, but they did nothing to stop the smuggling. Why? They were making good coin from it.

I knew what Humvees were before Pax spelled it out it for me. But I didn't know how dangerous they are. They look pretty tough but they're not safe. For Afghanistan anyway. One of the Taliban's favorite weapons was IEDs, bombs they'd make on their own and hide along the roadside, waiting for a Humvee to drive over it, when they'd set it off.

Turns out the flat bottom of the Humvees makes the explosion even worse, because it absorbs the impact of the bomb instead of deflecting it. I saw a ton of pics of Humvees that were completely trashed. They looked like they were blown up from the inside out.

The Army said its strategy back then was to "win the hearts and minds of the people," so there were a lot of rules about when and where we could fight. It makes sense, but the Taliban figured out the rules and used them to their advantage.

They knew their men were safe in the villages as long as they didn't carry any weapons. So they kept their guns and ammo hidden. During the day they went about their business, like normal times. Then at night they'd go get their weapons, load up, and set up their attacks, like mortar and sniper attacks on the fort, or ambushes on the patrols along the road.

You'd think the local people would turn the bad guys in, but we didn't get a lot of cooperation from them. Either the people were afraid of the Taliban or didn't want our help to begin with. Maybe they did once, but just got sick of us being there.

Some veterans dedicated their sites to friends who never made it home. I read about one unit who were really tight. One night, two of the guys volunteered for a mission they knew could be dangerous. They went out with a couple of Afghan scouts who said they could take them to a stash of weapons. They took them to some guns all right—ones pointed directly at them. They walked right into an ambush.

The blogs remind me of what my dad wrote. I've seen plenty of war movies, but it's just not the same as what I'm reading. In the movies, sometimes you feel like you're right there with the guys, feeling fear during an attack, anger when someone gets hit, sad when someone dies. But it's only temporary—soon enough you notice something that brings you back to your reality, like the red lights that show you the way down the aisle and out the door.

The veterans' stories are different. They can be hard to follow. There are misspellings and bad grammar and lots of jargon, but you get the point. They describe what happened to them, and a lot of times there's no happy ending or even a moral to the story. It's like they don't know what it means, but it's important, so they capture as many details as they can and maybe try to put it together later. They do seem to figure out one thing pretty quick. Even if you are lucky enough to come home, after all you've been through, you don't come home the same as when you left.

I look up at the TV and I'm shocked to see it's already halftime. I'm not surprised to see the score, though. The commentator is going off about how the Celts are down twenty to a team that should be in the G League. But I don't care—if they don't, why should I?

I've had enough for the night. I kill the TV, put my phone aside, and get ready for bed.

Even after OT turns his TV off, I still can't chill enough to fall asleep. Thoughts of my dad and my bro keep bubbling up to fill my head. I wonder how much Afghanistan changed my dad. I wouldn't know, because I didn't know him from before, but Pax did. Did he see a difference?

Then there's Pax himself. They say people who forget history are gonna repeat it. From what he's writing in the journal, he seems like he's ready to give war another shot. If he goes and signs up to fight, how different will he be when he gets home? If he even makes it back.

My phone buzzes on the floor next to me and I reach over to check it. Is my bro finally getting back to me? I wish. It's just the final score from the Celtics game. They lost!

Eight

It's just me and my homeroom desk again. I'm first in class, just sitting here, vibing on my beats, listening to Post Malone. It's too bad Pax never got into him, because Post dropped some wisdom in Jonestown he could use. Like the people in that cult found out, if you just go and drink the Kool-Aid like your leader says, you might wind up dead.

Coach walks in after a few minutes and nods to me like it's perfectly normal to see me sitting by myself in an empty classroom. He must think I'm putting in 100% in school like I did in open gym the other night. I guess my grades have picked up since OT made it clear that basketball is on the line.

The class slowly filters in and I try not to pay much attention to anyone. I barely even look up when Wick walks in. I'm starting to wonder if I blew it the other night. Maybe I should have played my own game after all. It sounds like that's what Babyman Maguire wants to see.

The way it went down, I gave buckets away. Fine, I got plenty of assists, and if you were paying attention you saw that, but how much did the coaches really see? They had two games to watch. If all they saw was the ball going through the basket, then Wick looked as good as me, maybe even better, because he never showboats, and some coaches don't like that kind of stuff.

The sight of Lea coming down the row shakes me out of my funk. She always gets my attention. She moves as quick as she usually does but gives me a look as she passes by. I'll take a shot of her sky blue eyes any day of the week, no matter how brief it is!

Coach perks up after the pledge and stands at the front of the class. We're starting with English today so we're staying here. He reaches a long arm around the smartboard and powers it on without having to move his feet. It opens to the president's latest tweet storm. I don't even bother to read it. I see all the capital letters and the exclamation points and I'm good. I'm sure there's nothing new there.

He flashes me a quick look, probably trying to make sure I'm not freaking out over the tweets, then launches into his spiel. "OK, everyone, we've been talking about communications," he starts. "Let's dig a little deeper today. A lot of people say no one reads any more, but if you look close, you'll find that there are hidden stories all around us, ones we see every day. You just have to know how to break them down.

"First, let's do a quick review of where we are," he says, folding his arms in front of him, in his standard coach's pose, like he's done his part in preparing us and now it's time see what we've got. "What modes of communication have we looked at?"

"Twitter, of course," Wick says from his corner of the room. "It's right there on the smartboard."

"Master of the obvious, as usual," Coach says with a laugh. "But thanks for getting us started. What story elements do you see there?"

"The president's tweets are always about himself," Lea says from way behind me. "He's the main character." She's so many rows back, I can't see her without doing a one-eighty, so I have to use my imagination instead. I've got to get myself in the back row one of these years. Teachers usually put me in the front, even though kids complain that my dreads block their view.

"Good. And the main character, the protagonist, needs a goal, right?"

"To make America number one again." It's Wick again. Like him and Lea are teaching the class.

"And that's where it gets interesting, right?" Coach asks. "No goal worth achieving is easy, so there's always some tension involved. There will be an obstacle, something blocking the protagonist from reaching the goal. The obstacle can be internal, something about your own self, or external, another person or thing. When it's another character, it's called the antagonist. Everyone got it?"

We nod our heads slowly.

"OK, then where is the tension in the president's goal?"

I jump in to give us all a break from the Wick and Lea show. "It's the president's enemies, everyone trying to block America from being number one again."

"Of course! And when it comes to the president, there are a lot of enemies, right?"

What's Coach saying...I took the easy question? What's that all about? Maybe next time I'll just keep my mouth shut.

"All right," he says. "Enough talking for now. Let's do something with this information. We've got this one example down, now let's move on and look for other stories, and break them down in the same way."

The kids start to groan like he asked us to run suicides. Coach smiles like he wishes he could.

"Don't worry, I'll give you some help. You can work with a partner. How about each group finds another hidden story, identifies the elements, and then brings it back to the class? OK?"

Wick looks over at me, like we'll dominate this together. I hate to say it, but I'd rather work with someone else today. At some point, I've got to show everyone I don't need him.

He starts over and I'm scrambling to think up an excuse when Coach stops him cold. "Hold up a sec," he says, extending his hands like he's holding him back. "Where are you going?"

"I'm going to get a partner."

"We're going to do random partners today."

Wick freezes. Maybe Coach is thinking what I'm thinking. It might be better for both of us this way. Well, better for me anyway.

Coach goes back to his desk, looks down at the class list, and starts calling out names in pairs. Wick ends up with Lea, which is a pretty nice consolation prize. And I get Rodrigo. What are the odds of that? I kind of doubt it was a random choice.

Rodrigo turns his desk to face mine and smacks the two of them together. Hard. He's lucky I don't flop like he did and lay out on the floor.

"What up, nerd?" he says.

"You serious? Nerd? Do nerds usually dominate you in hoops?"

"You talking about open gym?" he asks, narrowing his eyes and doubling up his unibrow. "That was two-on-one, you and your boy against me, and I still held my own. I heard tomorrow is gonna be a way different format."

"I hope so. Because I have a lot more to show."

"Hey guys," Coach shouts from the front of the room, looking our way. "I'm glad you're working on your social skills, you definitely need help there, but can you get to the project?"

"Yeah, sorry," I say, then turn back to Rodrigo.

He pulls his phone from his pocket and starts poking at it. "Yo, you seem to have this down. What else you got?"

"This is supposed to be a group project. I'm not doing all the work."

He drops his hand and shoots me a hard look. "So, we need a story. You got any ideas?"

I look over at the phone. It's open to NBA All the Way. "Yeah, actually. Let's go with that."

He doesn't get it. "What you talking about?"

"That game on your phone. We both know hoops. This should be an easy one for us."

"You serious? I don't see no...protagonist here."

I'm surprised he's not feeling it. Maybe it's because hoops is just about all I think about, but it seems so obvious to me. "Who are you?"

"Rodrigo. Basketball superstar. You know all about it."

"No, I mean in the game."

"Yeah, I'm me."

"Oh OK, I get it." He means he created a character for the game, one based on himself. "You created a character."

"Yeah, me."

"And do you have a goal?"

"Yeah, to get whatever this is, over with."

"No, in the game."

"Isn't it obvious? To win the MVP."

"Not to win the championship?" I'm not sure why that surprises me, but it does.

"Yeah, that too, of course, I want an MVP, All Star appearance, Finals MVP, Hall of Fame, all of that."

"OK, you want to bring your team to the Finals, win it, and take home the MVP trophy." The Finals MVP always comes from the winning team. It wouldn't make sense otherwise.

"Yeah, what I said."

"OK. We've got a character—your character in the game, a goal—winning the championship. So what's the conflict...it's easy, right?"

"Yeah, all the chumps getting in my way."

"OK, and who is that specifically?"

"Man, why I doing all the work here?"

"OK, fine, it's basically everyone else in the game who isn't on your team, right? Other players, other teams, other GMs, and on down the line."

"That's not very specific. How about I got to the Finals, and there's just one more team in my way?"

"And you called me the nerd?"

"Just saying."

"What team you on?"

"The Lakers."

"You serious?" I don't know if I can run with those guys. Our project felt like it was about done, but now it's gonna break down.

"Yeah, I love the purple and gold. Always have."

"And who is your opponent?"

"The Celtics."

"No way!" That's literally the worse thing he could say!

"Hey, they got there, too. It had nothing to do with me. I play my own character and let the computer take care of everyone else."

I don't even want to ask my next question. "We need an obstacle. Maybe it's you? You have a flaw in your game you have to overcome?"

"No way. The antagonist will be the best player on the other team, obviously Jayson Tatum."

The kid's killing me with this stuff! I've got to remember, it's just a game, and even then, there's no guarantee he's going to accomplish his goal, beating the Celtics and taking the Lakers to the promised land. Especially if he plays hoops in the video game anything like he does in real life.

So I have to go with it. We wrap it up and plan out our presentation. Rodrigo takes screen grabs of himself in the video game, in his dumbass Lakers jersey, going one-on-one with Tatum, all of that, and we get them ready to share on the smartboard.

Coach picks us to present to the class first. Of course. Rodrigo goes right into connecting his phone to the smartboard so he can pull up his pictures, and takes his sweet time at it, leaving me standing in front by myself. So of course, I have to do the talking. All of a sudden, I'm breathing harder than I was in the open gym. I'm surprised, because I usually don't mind when all eyes are on me, but whatever.

I decide to keep it simple and break each element down one by one. Rodrigo brings up his pics on the smartboard as I talk about them, adding background noises, like booing when Celtics appear— even Payton Pritchard, who no one has a problem with—and of course, ooh-ing and aah-ing when the Finals and MVP trophies are shown.

It ends up going pretty fast and it's over before I know it. When I finish, Coach puts his hands together and gets everyone clapping for us. People actually seem like they mean it. I think I even see a little extra sparkle in Lea's eyes.

No one seems as impressed as Rodrigo, though. He actually gives me dap when we finish. "That was fun, yo," he says as we head back to our desks.

On the flip side, Wick raises an extreme eyebrow when I get back. He's pretty much incredulous. Like, really? Rodrigo's the hero? Tatum's the bad guy? The only thing I can do is shrug at him.

Nine

Coach isn't in his classroom at the end of the school day, so I go by the coaches' offices on my way out, hoping to find him there. I actually want to thank him for putting me with Rodrigo. I wasn't feeling it at first, but I have to admit it worked out. And I want to make sure Coach remembers that. He needs to know I can work with Rodrigo in the classroom and on the court, too.

The coaches' offices are in a narrow walkway that connects the main school building to the gym. The place is like a dark tunnel, the walls painted the same deep red as the basketball courts, without even any windows to bring in more light. I'm always spooked when I walk through. I'm also on high alert in case a coach pops out and catches me doing something stupid.

My spidey-sense starts tingling before I get to the door so I kill my tunes just in case. It's a good thing, too, because as soon as I do, I hear Coach drop my name.

"If Noel and Wick decided to work together, I didn't have anything to do with it." Coach sounds like he's on the defensive.

"I'm just saying, if anyone did, it's against the rules." The other voice belongs to Coach Maguire, who sounds much more aggressive.

They're not exactly fighting, but there's definitely tension in the air. "You can't organize kids before the tryouts start."

I stop dead in my tracks and slide to the side of the hallway. I've got to know what this is all about. I take my phone out so it looks like I'm just killing time, waiting for the coaches to finish their talk, and giving them space to do it. I'm a little too close to the janitor's closet next door for comfort and all I can smell is the sharp scent of disinfectant. That's OK because I can hear every word they say—it's not my fault coaches always project their voices!

"You know they played together at the Y, right?" Coach asks.

"You saw what happened. It looked like way more than two kids who'd played together in the past. It was two kids playing together in the present. They were running plays for each other out there."

Leave it to the Babyman to make a positive into a negative. So he noticed that me and Wick can make each other better. What's wrong with that?

"Well, we're building a team here, right? Don't we want the kids to work together? If two of them are already doing it, aren't we ahead of the game?"

I appreciate the way Coach has our back. Maybe Maguire will head off into the sunset after a few more years, and when we're ready for varsity, Coach will move right up with us. Then again, maybe Coach leveling up and taking his spot is what he's worried about.

"No, we aren't," Maguire says. "Because it gets in the way of our evaluation of each player as an individual. When kids work in pairs, they could be covering for each other, covering their weaknesses."

Weaknesses? Is that what he thinks we're doing? Covering for each other? I feel like stepping inside the office and asking that chump what weaknesses I have in my game. That soft bastard is the one who's weak!

"Look, I'm not trying to big boy you here." It's Maguire again. "I made it clear when you took the role, right? It's my program, and you may be coaching the freshman team, but I'll be picking the players. You can't just move your players from the Y over to Holloway High."

Ouch—I didn't see that coming. I figured Coach would be picking his own team. Maguire making the cuts could be a problem for me. The thing is, he arrived at Holloway High when Pax was a junior. So Maguire might measure me against him instead of the other kids in the tryouts. Which is totally unfair because he didn't even know my brother when he was a freshman.

"I haven't forgotten that," Coach says. It sounds like he's backpedaling.

"In a way, you could take it as a compliment," Maguire says, lowering the volume a bit, now that he has Coach on the run. "Your kids obviously learned to play together. But, in the long run, those kids having played for you might hurt them more than help them."

"What do you mean?"

"Well, I've got to wonder how much better they are going to get under you? For example, think about Rodrigo. He's super-talented but doesn't always play the right way. I might expect you to change that. The way I'm looking at it, while some of the kids that played for you might have a higher floor, Rodrigo may have a higher ceiling. You may have already gotten the best out of your kids. What if they're actually at their peak right now? And who knows how much better Rodrigo can get?"

"How would you know that? Don't you typically evaluate kids based on what they show you?"

"Yes, of course. But you have to use what you see to make a projection. I'm not saying your kids don't have a shot. They do, obviously. In a way, they caught a break, because a couple of your players went away to prep school. If the bald kid came out, and that little black kid too, then you'd be in a tough spot. So their chances are better than they otherwise might be. But they have to earn it. On their own. Without help from you. Or each other."

A couple of girls in volleyball short-shorts come through on their way to the gym and I miss Coach's comeback. The way they bounce their balls off the floor as they run, low and hard, with both hands, makes the sound echo around the tight hallway.

As much I'd like to stay and see the rest of the team run by too, I have to beat it before I get caught snooping. I've heard enough anyway.

I pivot and head back to the main building, wondering what Maguire's plan is for the next open gym. What is he going to do with me and Wick? Just some boring drills? A skills competition? Scrimmages with us on opposite teams?

Wick says we're not competing against each other, but Maguire sounds like he wants to set it up that way. We showed up and showed out the other night! He should be gassing us up, not cutting us down. The way I see it, we should have the team made already. Instead, it looks like we'll be going head-to-head.

Ten

The message pops up on my phone without making a sound—I put it in silent mode to cut down on my interruptions—but even that isn't working:

Yo bro. Taking care of business. How about you?

At least Pax is finally getting back to me. Still, it's taken him 24 hours to respond to a simple what you up to? What's that all about? I kind of feel like making him wait too, but I decide against it. I don't play games like that.

Same old, I text back.

I slide the journal back under my bed, then go back to lounging. That's right—I'm keeping the book in my room now. This way I don't have to wait until OT leaves to get some reading in.

I heard you made quite an impression on Coach, he says.

At first, I think he's talking about the presentation me and Rodrigo did in Coach's English class. Then I remember that to him, Coach is Coach Maguire.

Who said that?

You have to know good reporters don't reveal their sources. Or did your coach-turned-English teacher not teach you that yet? Or do I have it wrong? Did he actually become a janitor?

I'm gonna ignore that shot at Coach. For some reason, he's never been a fan. Like it's his fault we struggled my first few seasons at the Y. But I know better. Coach had us prepared. I think Babyman Maguire knows better, too. It's probably why he's so afraid of us Blazers taking over his program.

We only had one open gym, I answer. *Me and Wick felt good about it, but we know it's early.*

I don't mention how we stood out because we worked together, and how that's not going to work next time, because Maguire plans to break us up.

Just keep it up. You have eyes on you.

You talking to one of the seniors? I ask. *Or Babyman Maguire himself?*

What? Babyman? Where did that come from?

I'm thinking his big fat mama.

You better call him Coach Maguire, he corrects me. *And I told you I'm not revealing my sources.*

Enough about me, I text back. I'm not really in the mood to be lectured about things at home by someone a thousand miles away anyway. *You know what I'm up to. What are you up to? You still in Florida? Or can't you say, now that you're some kind of investigative reporter?*

Yeah, I'm doing some investigating all right, he texts back, adding an emoji of a Sherlock Holmes-looking character with a huge magnifying glass.

Investigating what?

Man, you do have an inquiring mind, don't you! I'm checking out a few situations down here.

Does he mean jucos? From what I heard, junior colleges are for kids whose grades aren't good enough for four-year schools. But Pax's grades and SATs were plenty good enough, according to the U, anyway.

I get up and take a walk over to my little window and admire my view of the U's gym. Well, its roof anyway. Past all the condo roofs, I can see the sun reflecting off the metal flashing along the top.

We had some good times in that gym and could have had a lot more if Pax went there. Coach took us to a few games. The gym is really small, and they don't have a lot of fans, so there isn't much going on in the stands. Coach loved that, because it means you can see and hear everything that happens on the court. The coaches instructing the players, the players talking to each other, the coaches and players giving it to the refs. It's constant communication out there, a game within a game, but in bigger arenas, with more fans, the crowd noise usually blocks it out.

If Pax played at the U, I could probably go to some games for free. Never mind Mario and his Celtics tickets...I'd have my own swag to distribute. And an athlete like Lea would have to be impressed by that.

You wouldn't have to be doing all this investigating if you took the offer you had on the table.

And live at home? How am I gonna become the best man I can if I live under OT's roof?

Become the best man he can—what's that? Some kind of military slogan? He might be looking at more than jucos down there. Maybe recruiting centers, too. That is, if he's even in Florida. He could be at boot camp right now, for all I know. I've been dying to check his location, but he might have alerts set up for that, and if he caught me I'd look like some kind of freak.

OT's not that bad, I text back.

You know he's easier on you than me. The older he gets, the softer he gets.

I wouldn't call him soft. Especially if I were a guy who admires Babyman Maguire.

It's all relative, you know what I mean. Besides you have nothing to compare it to. I'm the one who remembers living with our mom and dad.

The tree across the street catches my eye. Some burnt-looking leaves attached to the branches are twisting in the wind. They're all dried up and curled in on themselves, but somehow they're still hanging on.

We're lucky he took us in.

No doubt. I was just saying. Complaining, I guess. My bad. So how is the big fella anyway?

He's good. Auntie called the other day and asked if he was taking his meds.

Good, just make sure you check from time to time. He needs his meds to keep that heart of gold going strong. He adds a cheesy smiling emoji.

I got it. So why did you pick Florida anyway?

What's wrong with Florida? There's a lot going on down here.

I know, especially after the October Surprise.

Word. I drove by Magicland the other day just to check it out. It's still closed. They put up this big fence around it and you can't see anything inside. All you see is guys in hazmat suits coming and going. The air smells funny, too, like it's still burning in there. Hard to believe we forgot. That we let it happen again.

Now he even sounds like a reporter. Or an editorial writer. Never mind jucos, maybe he should be looking at journalism schools down there.

Why would you want to drive by that place anyway?

You know this is history, right?

Talking about history, I've got a question to ask. I might regret it, but I have no idea when I'm going to talk to him again.

I've been reading Dad's journal. You too, right? Those your notes?

You're reading that? I don't remember leaving that out for public consumption.

Public consumption? Is he serious? It's not like it's his personal property. I'm his dad's kid, too. It's not my fault Pax left his sloppy handwriting all over it like it's his own diary.

OK. I guess I should have given it to you. So you didn't have to find it on your own like I did.

True that. It seems like some kind of weird family secret.

Yeah, that bothered me at first, too. Now I kind of understand. It's really never done anyone good.

What do you mean?

The only one I really know that read it for sure is Mom. I asked OT about it, and he dodged it big time. He obviously knew it existed, but I don't know if he knew what was in it. Just gave me an "end of discussion" and that was it.

I look back at my bed and see part of the journal cover poking out. I go over and push it all the way under so it's hidden again. Like everyone else, I guess.

When did Mom read it? Before she left?

Seems like it.

Does it get bad? Is that why she left? Is that why you're so judgmental about it?

Whoa, hold up a sec. Talking about sources, it's time for me to talk to someone. I've got to go. Keep reading and we'll keep talking.

Are we talking? It doesn't feel like we talk much lately.

Maybe we can talk in person. When are you coming back?

Soon. Really? Does that mean no military for him?

How soon?

That I don't know. I've got to finish my investigation. He adds a winking smiley.

OK.

Don't worry. I'll be back. I'm not going anywhere.

That sounds good, but the way the president is talking, whether or not Pax goes anywhere may not be totally up to him.

Eleven

With all the surreptitious hoops stuff that's going on at school, I'm not surprised when Coach Brady, the JV coach and PE teacher, announces that we'll be playing basketball golf in gym class. I don't even know exactly what basketball golf is, but I have a feeling it's just another way for the coaches to get a look at our games.

Mario, the kid with the least game, is the one who acts like he's offended. "Basketball and golf? They don't have anything in common! One is street and one is country club."

"Hold on, hold on," Brady says, waving his stubby little arms in front of him. It doesn't help Brady's credibility that he's so short and fat. The guy looks even less athletic than Maguire. He could probably pass for the Babyman's baby brother. I guess that would make him Babyboy. Babyman and Babyboy—that's quite the coaching tandem!

"Give me a chance to walk you through it," he says, then turns to the court and waits for our eyes to follow his. It's set up with three cones at every basket, like a series of shooting stations. It's obviously part of Maguire's master plan to single us out. He wants Brady to identify who the shooters are and report back.

"The goal of both basketball and golf is to put the ball in the bucket, whether it's the hoop or the cup, right? So the basketball part of our game involves you shooting from the spots on the floor marked by the cones."

I nod my head, realizing I was right. This is a shooting drill. Out of the corner of my eye I see Rodrigo look my way and raise his brow, like he thinks I knew it was coming all along and I'm ready for it. This school is making us all paranoid.

"OK so far?" Brady says. "Now here's where the golf part of the game comes in. Golfers play eighteen holes, right? Well, with three cones at each basket, and six baskets in the gym, you'll have eighteen chances to score."

He raises his little arms again to stop Mario from voicing his next objection. I'm not sure when the kid became the class spokesman for basketball. Come to think of it, I don't even remember seeing him at open gym. I guess he's feeling full of himself with the Celtics-Lakers game coming up.

"We'll score the game the same way golf does," Brady goes on. "Each cone has an index card attached to it, and on the card is a number, which is the par for the shot. Par is golf-speak for how many shots it would take an average player to finish a hole. Each cone represents either a par one, two, or three, depending on your distance from the hoop. The farther the shot, the higher the par. So, a three-point shot is a par three, because an average player would need three shots to make one. A regular field goal is a par two and a layup is a par one. You just have to subtract the par from the number of shots it actually takes to figure your score. And record it on a scorecard I'll give you. Make sense?"

"We all know how you score ones, twos, and threes in basketball," Mario says, ignoring all that complicated stuff Brady just laid on us. I'm guessing he's had enough talk. "So where are the balls? Don't we need to warm up?"

"If you had the basketballs right now, I wouldn't be able to hear myself think over the dribbling, never mind explain this to you," Brady answers. "Besides, we don't have the time to warm up. We've got to finish this course in a single class."

Now I'm the one who feels like objecting. Without giving us time to get loose, this won't be an accurate test of our shooting ability, especially for a streaky shooter like me. I'm either hot or cold, and if I'm cold, I need more shots to get back on track. It also means Wick is going to have a major advantage over me because of those shooting camps of his. His technique is more consistent than mine these days.

Brady announces the teams and just like you'd expect, he spreads the talent out across the gym. He assigns me, Wick, and Rodrigo to different teams, not to mention a few other kids who can play, too. It's obvious he wants to be able to keep an eye on each of us while making it look like he's watching the whole class. Never mind that he's going to have scorecards to track our performance...he wants to see as much as possible with his own eyes.

My teammates are Mario and Lea, so it looks like I'm going to be up against it. Mario might get sweet tix to C's games, but he's no Super Mario, that's for sure. I don't know much about golf, but I know what a handicap is, and he's mine. I'm not sure about Lea. She's an athlete, but I've never seen her play.

Lea takes charge as soon as we gather. "I'll be our scorer," she says.

"You sure?" I ask. I love her confidence, but it seems a little unrealistic. "Nothing personal, but I planned on doing most of the scoring."

"Actually, that would be me," says Mario. "I'm about to put on a three-point barrage."

"Are you serious?" Lea asks him. "We all know Noel is our resident superstar." It sounds like she's had enough of his act, too. "Anyway, what I meant was, I'll keep score. My dad golfs all the time and I used to go with him to score his games when I was a kid. I'll go over and grab a scorecard and get us a ball."

She turns and marches over to Brady to collect our supplies while me and Mario watch her go.

"What an attitude!" he says. "And to think I almost picked her for the game."

"She sign your sheet?" I ask. I'd be surprised if she did.

He gives me a sideways look, like he's not sure how he should answer. "No," he says, picking the truth. I've got to give the girl props—she continues to impress.

"All right boys," Lea says when she gets back, dropping the ball and starting to pencil in our names on the scorecard. "Time to see what you got."

Mario scoops up the ball and starts dribbling around the first hoop like a madman. Never mind helping his shooting with a warmup, he looks like he's more likely to hurt it by injuring himself.

"Hey, I liked the presentation you did with Rodrigo the other day," Lea says, taking her eyes off Mario's clown act only long enough to flash a quick look at me.

Mario starts shooting at the cone closest to the basket. And missing. And shooting and missing some more.

"I know you'd rather have worked on that project with Wick," she says. "It was pretty funny watching with him, because every time Rodrigo shared a screen capture from his game, Wick had something to say. He basically had a running commentary going the whole time."

What, he was running me down to Lea? That's not cool!

"Hey, I'm no Lakers fan," I say. "But the story basically wrote itself. I was hoping Rodrigo would be his own enemy, like he had to overcome some part of his game to achieve his goals, but he wouldn't go for it."

She laughs. "Wick was pointing out plenty of his shortcomings, that's for sure."

"Our story was the same way," Mario says, coming over to retrieve the ball after dribbling it off his foot. "It was right there on the smartboard."

Mario's story was about the president announcing the firing of an aide for leaking information to the press. He did it on Twitter. That was pretty cold.

"You could've used a little more critical analysis," Lea says, shooting him a serious look. "You pretty much took the president's tweet directly from the smartboard."

"We thought it was pretty deep," Mario answers.

"What would've been deep is if you looked a little closer," Lea says. "If you told the story from the aide's point of view. He found out the president was basically lying with all his tweets about new terrorist threats, and he had to decide whether to choose loyalty to the country or loyalty to the president."

"That's your opinion," Mario says. "It was basically one guy's word against another. You just picked the one that agreed with your politics."

"I picked the one who isn't already a proven liar," Lea answers.

"Whatever," Mario says, and goes back to shooting. Well, missing.

"So you think what happened to Magicland is fake news?" I ask. The last thing I want to do is get into politics, but that would be kind of crazy.

"No, of course not," she says, turning her serious look on me. "I just think the president is making things worse. His whole goal is to boost his popularity in time for the next election. The problem is, by talking up these terrorist groups, he's boosting their popularity, too. That gives them more followers, more funds, and makes it more likely there will be another attack."

Brady calls across the gym. "Lea and Noel, can you get to know each other better in another, less important, class?"

A couple kids laugh, including Mario, even though he's the one that started the whole thing. I need to take a break from Lea and get my head in the game. Not only is Brady gonna be watching me, but the way he called me and Lea out, everyone else in the gym is gonna be checking on us, too.

Mario knows our team is in the spotlight, so he wants the ball out of his hands. He flips it over to me and when I catch it, I realize how cold my hands are. I can barely feel the ribbing on the ball, never mind the dimples. I've got to stop letting politics get in the way of my game.

The nearest cone to me is the par 3. With everyone looking my way, I'm not gonna walk past it and take an easier shot. It'll make me look like I have no confidence. If there's one thing I know, it's that you can't show doubt on a basketball court. If you don't believe in yourself, who else will?

So I let it fly and the ball somehow comes off my fingertips nice and soft. It rolls around the rim a few times, teasing everyone, then drops down and through. I held my shooting pose the whole time for everyone to appreciate.

"That's a hole in one!" Lea says it super loud, so the whole gym can hear it.

Apparently they did, because Brady answers from across the way. "That's our first of the day," he says. "Let's see who else can match it."

I watch as Lea writes out my name on the card and adds a -2 under it. I knew the scoring system sounded goofy, but I didn't expect to have a negative score.

"Shouldn't that be worth three points?"

"The cones was a par three, and you made it in one stroke, so you're a negative two."

It sounds backwards to me. What is this, opposite world? And what is Maguire gonna think when he sees it on the scorecard?

"In golf, low score wins," she says. "You have a perfect score so far."

"That was nothing," says Mario. "Watch me match it."

He steps right up and airballs a three. Lea looks at me and rolls her eyes.

"You think you can do better?" Mario asks. He gets the rebound and throws her the ball.

"It won't be hard," she says, stepping up to the cone. "All I have to do is hit the rim."

But she doesn't. She throws the ball up hard and it hits the backboard and comes right back to her. Another ugly miss.

They both laugh, but I'm not feeling it. Despite my negative score, they've put us right back on the positive side, which according to Lea is a bad thing. Our team score goes from my -2 to a +4. There probably isn't even a word for that in golf-speak.

The only thing I can do is go to the two easier cones and make those shots. I do and at least we're trending in the right direction again.

"Now that, I know I can match," Mario says, then retraces my footsteps, and misses both shots. Maybe this really is opposite world, because he keeps cancelling me out. Between the two of us, we're now a zero.

Lea goes last. Her technique on her first shot, another miss, isn't that great, so I try to get her to watch me and imitate my form. When I tell her to lower her butt, she goes from serious to suspicious, like I'm trying to get her to do something dirty. Then Mario slides behind her to watch and she gives up.

She actually makes the par 2, but misses the par 1. So our overall team score really is a zero.

We rotate to the next basket and I start at the par 3 again. Mario appears at my side at the last second and blocks my shot. What a noodge! I grab the ball back and try to take another shot, but Brady is all over it. "One shot at each cone," he calls over.

Lea gives Mario a dirty look, like, what's that all about? I feel like actually doing something about it, but with Brady watching me so close, I know I have to swallow my pride and suck it up. I don't want to get a reputation for having an anger management problem.

I keep an eye on Mario as I take the two easy shots, making both.

When it's Mario's turn to shoot, I think about blocking him in revenge, then I realize there's no need. It's more fun to watch him miss on his own. Especially when he'd probably rather have me to try to block his shot so he'd have an excuse.

Lea makes one out of three again.

At the next basket, Mario reaches from behind me and tickles my underarm as I shoot it. I'm already in my motion when I feel his cold little fingers and shoot another airball. I look over to Brady, hoping he'll somehow bail me out, but his attention is on another group. I'm tempted to take another shot while he's not looking, but Mario is so annoying he'd probably rat me out. What's his problem today, anyway?

Lea gets right up in Mario's grill. "You know we're on the same team, right?" she asks.

He's not exactly intimidated by her. The smile on his face says he's actually loving every second of it.

I walk over too and show him my game face, death stare edition, and he actually gulps as he looks away. "Sorry, won't happen again," he says.

Brady finally calls it after everyone has gone through five baskets. We didn't even get through our 18 holes. Oh well. I've had enough.

Lea does the math and our team score is a 32. We've got to be in last place. Individually, we're all on the wrong side of zero. I get a 5, Mario a 14, and Lea a 13.

"Bro, I can't believe I beat you," Mario says. "I actually outscored you!"

"Having more points is not a good thing," I counter. "You actually finished last. Like you deserved."

"Lowest score wins, you dumbass," Lea says. "If you hadn't messed with two of his threes, Noel was on track for a perfect score."

Those misses are all I can think of when we hand in our score. I made three but missed two, once when Mario blocked it and the other when he tickled me. So when it comes to threes, I finished with a zero. You know Maguire is going to be all over it—and I doubt he'll hear anything about Mario's sabotage either.

Twelve

Pax's only comment on my dad's latest journal entry rings in my ears as I get loose at the next open gym:

Sounds like you needed that R&R.

Tonight, me and Wick are keeping our distance, hoping Maguire forgot about breaking us up, not about to do anything to help him remember. So this time I'm lost in my own little world like everyone else.

The journal entry that brought on my brother's one-liner went like this:

Dutch got hit by a sniper this morning on resupply duty. Shot in the head. Died instantly. The guys said his legs just went limp.

Tim (squad leader) asks me to join a small group heading higher up the valley to set up an observation post. It's dangerous because we'll be exposed, but someone has to do it.

It was real scary. I wasn't the only one who felt that way. Jim lit up a lot. We had to keep telling him to put it out. Jay was radio and talks all the time.

It was hard work. Took a few days to scratch fighting holes out of the rocky ground. Heard a deafening explosion on second day. Humvee destroyed by massive IED. Got on radio and learned Tim and Murphy got killed.

Got a package from Jenny. I should write to her but I don't know what to say. A strong feeling of indifference has come over me.

Observation post got hit at 4 a.m. RPG hit behind me—wounded me and 2 others. Medevacked to hospital to get fixed up. Going on R&R after that.

Laying around hospital, I have plenty of time to think. Which might be a bad thing. It's become obvious the people in Korengal don't want us there. When we patrol the villages, the children don't want to take our candy, the women won't look at us, the old men shoot us dirty looks out of the corner of their eyes. The young men look at us all right. With an "I'll see you later" type look. At the ambush!

They tell us our mission is to remove the Taliban from the valley. But how do we do that if the Taliban is the valley?

~ * ~

Boomer walks out to center court and pierces the air with his whistle to get the party started. "OK, listen up," he shouts, then pauses for the silence he knows is coming. We're hanging on his every word and you can tell he's really enjoying his new status.

"All right then," he finally says. "After watching you guys play the other night, it's obvious that, with a few rare exceptions, most of you think basketball is an individual game. So we've decided to roll with that to keep you comfortable. Tonight we're gonna have a one-on-one tournament."

The kids whoop it up and Boomer uses his whistle again to quiet everyone. I just hope I get lucky and I won't have to face Wick till the final round. Then the worst either of us could finish would be runner up.

"It'll be like March Madness," Boomer explains. "We've divided everyone up into brackets, and you'll play each other in a series of half-court games, eight minutes, running time. Each will be a single elimination game, so if you lose, you're out. We'll keep going until only one of you is left."

The kids make even more noise and the coaches use it as cover to sneak in the side door of the gym. Boomer just keeps on talking. "To make this fair, we've randomly picked the matchups. They're posted outside the office. Go check out your assignment and get yourself ready."

I take my time heading over, doing a dribble warmup, like I don't care who I play. Before I get there, a tall, skinny kid named Jon runs past me. "See you at hoop three," he says, with a cocky smile. I'm feeling kind of lost in my head, so that smile was just what I needed to get going.

I know Jon's game. He played outside at the U a few times this summer. He's pretty good, but he's also pretty slow. He never gave me a problem there and I'm not anticipating one here. Still, I'm not taking anything for granted. I burn the image of his arrogant smile into my memory to keep myself motivated. I look forward to erasing that smile during our game.

Boomer whistles yet again and tells us we'll start in two minutes. I take my time heading over to meet Jon. Steve, the senior who coached me and Wick the other night, is at the hoop, too. He's got a whistle around his neck, so I'm guessing he'll be our referee.

Steve explains the rules. We're playing twos and ones, "make it, take it," and we have to clear everything. Jon wins the coin toss, so he'll get the ball to start. I line up between him and the basket, knees bent, arms extended. Once he has the ball, he dribbles right at me. I back off to prevent a drive and he goes right into his shot. He drains it and it's 1-0 just like that.

Jon keeps the ball and sets up again at the top of the key. When you play "make it, take it" like this you maintain possession after you score, so a game can get out of hand fast if you can't get a stop. It's time to step up.

I swing my hands up and down in front of him, at times blocking his view with one hand and preventing a dribble drive with the other, then vice versa. I'm all over him like Spider-Man when he grew those four extra arms.

He rocks back, confused by all the movement, and I bring my hands together and rip the ball clean away. I take a couple quick dribbles out to the three-point line to clear the ball and then turn toward the hoop, making sure I keep my dribble going so I have all my options available to me.

Jon sets up on defense and I can tell from the look on his face that he's pissed about my steal. Already? The kid needs to work on his mental game. The way he's acting, I'm positive he'll go for the first good fake I give him.

I step to my right, then dribble between my legs and head left. He goes with my fake and gives me a clear path to the basket. I rush in and take the layup, using my left hand like I'm supposed to in case Maguire is watching. It's now 1-1.

Jon's not feeling so cocky anymore, so he lays back to prevent me from driving. That's fine with me, because I'll take the extra point they give you from deep. After seeing the show Wick put on last weekend, I've been working on my jumper too, shooting outside at the U all week. Fighting the cold and the wind, with no room for error, my shot has gotten nice and tight.

I go right into my shot without even bothering to give him a fake. It's all net. I'm up 3-1.

We check again and this time he plays me a little tighter. I juke right, then give him another crossover dribble. He doesn't go for my fake and slides back to block my lane to the hoop. His basketball brain is even slower than his body. He's defending what I've done already instead of what I've set him up to let me do next.

I step back and launch another deep shot. It catches the inside of the rim and spins around a little before falling through. I'm up 5-1 and he hasn't gotten close to bothering my shot.

I dribble around a while, trying to drain the clock and draw him outside, and when he decides he's had enough and comes out to meet me, I burst past him and go to the hole for an easy lay in. I'm up 6-1 as Steve whistles to end it. Time's up! I'm glad I'm moving on to the next round, but for once, I'm not about to act all that. I'm just getting started.

I head to my bag for a drink and look to see what's up with Wick. Turns out he was watching me play and I didn't even notice. Rodrigo, too. I don't know what to make of it until they walk onto the court after me. They're playing each other next. That's bad news. I might have to play Wick as early as the next round.

I take a walk to stay warm and because I don't want anyone to think I'm too interested in the result. I'm torn because I want Wick to win his game, but at the same time I don't want to face him. I try not to think about it at all. I need to keep it simple and play my game, regardless of who my opponent is.

After giving it some time, I head back to the court, only to see the game is tied at 10-all. It's a shootout! Wick has the ball and Rodrigo sets up in his crouch on defense, but he's giving up too much space. He's playing the old Wick, the player he was before he left for India and his shooting camps, the one without a jumper whose sole focus was going to the basket. Rodrigo is gambling that he doesn't have enough confidence in his outside shot to risk shooting from deep with the game on the line. Or maybe I'm overthinking it. Maybe Rodrigo is hanging back because he's wiped out.

Wick squares up, then goes into a step-back jumper to keep Rodrigo from getting anywhere near his shooting hand. He launches the ball with perfect technique and it sails slowly toward the basket. I know exactly what's going to happen the whole time. The ball meets the rim dead center and falls through the net without even rippling it.

That's it! It'll be me and Wick next. I jump on the court to get a few shots up while he goes for a drink. I know I wanted to play Wick one-on-one at the Y, but I don't have a good feeling about matching up here. The stakes are high and the coaches are gonna be all over it.

I'm getting lost in my head again and I've got to find an edge quick. Then it hits me that this whole thing is Wick's fault. If he hadn't come up with that stupid plan, about how we'd somehow help each other make the team, we wouldn't have targets on our backs, and we wouldn't have to square off like this.

I call heads and catch a break when I win the toss. It's my ball first. Wick sets up on defense and slaps his hands like he's ready for me, which seems kind of unnecessary. A little enthusiasm is fine, but still, it's me he's playing against, not some random kid. And we don't need any more drama over here on court #3. We got plenty enough already.

He might be showing some energy, but he has to be feeling a little laggy from just finishing a game. I decide to start inside, play ground-and-pound, and wear him down even more. I back him down with my dribble, but I'm starting to worry that he's going to pull the chair out from under me like I love to do. I don't want to end up on the floor.

I don't get anywhere near as close to the basket as I should and when I back-pivot into my jumper I find myself about 10 feet out. Worse, he's so close to me I go into a fall away, making the shot even harder. It lands a little short, catching the front of the rim and bouncing back weakly, right into his hands.

Now it's my turn to guard him. I know my length bothers him, so I play it conservative and just stay in front of him as he dribbles between his legs, back and forth, back and forth, trying to get me off balance. I know what he's trying to do, but it's still frustrating to just stand there and watch him dribble like it's a drill. It makes me feel kind of stupid.

When he catches me thinking, he blows by me and heads to the hoop. I recover quickly and trail him by only a half a step as he goes into his shot. He doesn't seem to realize it, but I'm still in the play. When he raises the ball from his waist to get it into a shooting position, I dart in and slap it away. It bounces off his knee and goes out of bounds. My ball again. It's my turn to clap my hands.

My baby cross-over worked against Jon, so I figure I'll try it on Wick. But Wick knows my moves, so I decide to add another between-the-legs dribble to get the ball back in my right hand. I catch him leaning and now it's my turn to go to the basket. I try to take advantage of the half step I have on him while I still have it by shooting a runner from about five feet out. It's farther out than I want to be, so I have to give it a little extra. I shoot it too strong and it ricochets off the backboard and goes to the other side of the court.

He beats me to the ball and turns to shoot immediately. He realizes too late that I stayed with the play and basically shoots it into my hand. It's an easy block. The ball lands out of bounds. We're both 0 for 2. And the score is still 0 to 0. No one watching is going to be impressed by anything they've seen so far.

My legs are feeling a little heavy, so I peek over at the clock. There are still five minutes to go. Then I notice something else—a ton of kids actually are watching. Everyone who got bounced in the first round seems to have decided this is the game to watch. Rodrigo seems especially interested. I guess he wins whether it's me or Wick that loses.

I look up at Wick and we make eye contact for the first time this game. He looks away fast. He's probably playing the same mental game as me. Or maybe not. When he sees I'm thinking again, he flies by me to the hoop. I follow him and try to slap the ball away like I did last time.

This time he takes better care of the ball. He shows it to me then hides it on the other side of his body. My slap hits him on the forearm and the sharp sound of flesh on flesh tells everyone in the gym it's a foul. It doesn't matter, because he made the shot, and there are no free throws in one-on-one anyway, but it still makes me look bad. Which I deserve. I put myself in such a bad position twice by thinking too much.

Now he's up 1-0. Some of the kids start to cheer. It pisses me off, because I know they're not rooting for someone to win, but they're rooting to lose. I need to do something special to shut them up.

Lucky for me I know the new Wick. He wants to show off his new touch and do some damage from outside. He wants to show everyone he doesn't have a one-dimensional game anymore.

He tries to take a step-back three like he did to end the game against Rodrigo, but I'm on it. I stuff it while it's still in his hand and end up with the ball.

I decide to show him I've got a game from distance, too. I spin like I'm going to back him down, then when I feel his forearm on my hip, I pivot away, plant both feet, and take my own deep jumper. It's as pretty as I hoped and the ball slices cleanly through the hoop.

It's 2-1. My ball, my lead, and the clock's ticking down. Wick is wary of my outside shot, so it's time to demonstrate once again that I own the paint. I put my head down and charge to the basket, determined to score the old-fashioned way and solidify my lead.

He stays right with me and I don't have much space to work with at all. I know I'm being stubborn, but I have to show the coaches how unstoppable I am regardless of the defense. I raise the ball up over my head and try to Euro step past him, stepping right then left and moving the ball from right to left as I do. But he's so close, my elbows give him a 1-2 combo in the head. He was waiting for the contact and snaps his head back like a boxer taking a knockout punch. He falls to the floor and I fall over him, too. I bang my elbow as I land and it hurts like a mother.

We're lying on the ground next to each other when Steve blows his whistle. I get up with the ball, assuming Steve knows what happened and is gonna call Wick for the foul. At this point, I'll just run out the clock.

Steve shocks me by thrusting his arm the other way. He's calling a charge on me. It's my foul, Wick's ball.

Out of the corner of my eye, I see Rodrigo cover his mouth in an "oh snap" and I realize Wick baited me into the whole thing. I throw the ball to him, right as he's trying to pick himself up. Problem is, his arms are underneath him, so he has no way to catch it. The ball nails him right in the head.

The kids watching us lose it. Steve jumps between me and Wick like he's breaking us up, even though we've barely moved. I hear a long whistle and look back to see Boomer coming over and pointing me and Wick to opposite ends of the gym.

I walk off the court all right—and don't stop until I'm outside the building. There's really no reason to stick around. I don't know what Maguire saw, and it doesn't really matter anyway. It's bad enough if he saw it and probably even worse if he didn't, because things like that get exaggerated the more they're talked about. Either way, I can probably kiss my chance of making the team goodbye.

Thirteen

Pax doesn't have a thing to say after the next section of the journal and I can't blame him:

Arrived at Qatar for R&R and got a room. Gene came in and said he had a girl for me. I was persistent in telling him no.

Spent the night in my room alone. Didn't call home or anything. I realize I'm not the same person that left the U.S. I don't know that I can go back and function in that life anymore. For myself or anyone else. Maybe Jenny and Pascal shouldn't know the new me. Maybe they'll be better off with their memories of the old me.

I see Gene at the bar the next night. Again I tell him no and go back to my room. He leaves and 10 minutes later there's a knock on the door—in she comes, the most beautiful little woman I have ever seen.

I wanted to get out of my room so we went to a movie. She was so fragile and tiny. I felt my emotions and senses slipping. I became more confused and scared. I didn't think about home or the war or anything—my mind just kept churning.

In the evening we went to another show. It was a thrill just to sit there with her and drink Cokes. We taught each other new words in our languages. I felt myself growing more and more fond of her, her deep brown eyes, long shiny black hair, button nose, and pouting lips.

I decided to stop fighting it.

By the time I have to leave, everything has changed. We make elaborate plans for the future and promise to write each other. I really think I am in love with her. If at all possible, I will come back and get her and we can live the life we planned.

Got up and went to R&R center to depart. Got my boarding pass number and stood outside with her till time to leave. It was hard to go back to Stan—I don't know whether it's because I love her or because I miss home.

I snap the book shut and let it go. It falls off the edge of the bed and drops to the carpet, the distressed cover facing up. Maybe it serves me right. What did I expect to find inside something that looks like that?

Not what I got. It's just too much. I understand that my dad was having a hard time. I get it. He just left a war zone where his buddies were dying around him. The people he was supposedly there to help made it clear they didn't want his help. It's a bad scene. It comes through loud and clear.

But cheating on my mom? Talking about not coming home when he got out? That's taking it to a whole different level. Fine, I'm not born yet, but he's got my mom. And Pax. Yet he's talking about abandoning everything.

Maybe it was just a bad moment, because in the end, he came home. He got himself together. And had me. But did he really want that life? Did he really want me? Would he have stayed with us if he hadn't got killed in that car crash?

OT picks the perfect moment to poke his head in the door. "You OK in here?" he asks.

The question fades from his eyes when he sees the journal on the floor. "Oh," he says. When he moves them up to lock onto mine, it's obvious he knows exactly what it is.

"Oh, yeah," I answer.

"You reading that?"

"I'm trying."

He comes over and sits on the edge of the bed. He sags when his butt hits it, curling into himself like one of the dried-out leaves on the tree outside.

"So...did you read it?" I ask.

His looks back to the journal and he slowly shakes his head no.

That's hard to believe, right? It seems like exactly the kind of thing you'd want to read, you know, your kid's experience in a war zone. Especially when you're all about proclaiming what a hero he was.

"How come?" I ask.

"It's hard to explain," he says.

Does he think it's none of his business? Like cracking it would be invading his kid's privacy or something? At some point it was locked shut. I didn't think twice about going through it, whether it was reading my dad's entries or even Pax's notes. Even when I had to sneak into Pax's room to get it. Maybe I should have.

"Didn't he want anyone to read it?" I ask. "I thought it was OK when I saw Pax..."

I stop myself before I finish, but it's already too late. If OT thinks this is private business, I just ratted out my brother for not respecting it.

"No, it's not that. You're not wrong to read it. Pascal wasn't wrong either."

"Then how come you didn't read it?"

"I...can't."

That doesn't sound like the tough guy I know. He can't take knowing what my dad went through? Shouldn't we know? It's hard for us, but wasn't it harder for him? Shouldn't we suck it up and get through it?

"Why not?" I ask. I feel like he should explain himself.

He looks over at me, his eyelids hanging halfway over his eyes. "I can't read."

All of a sudden it makes sense. Now I know why he doesn't need to wear his glasses all that much, why he needs help with his medicine. And why he's so tough on me about my grades.

"Sorry," I say. "I had no idea."

I feel bad, but then again, the only reason I didn't know was that he kept it secret. What is it with everyone in this family and their secrets?

"You don't have to apologize. I get by. I've always meant to learn. I will learn, believe me. But it takes time and it was never the most important thing."

Now I'm starting to feel guilty, because when he was supposed to have the time, when he could have retired and worked on something like that, he took me and Pax in, and once Gram died, he had to handle us by himself.

The thoughts in my head are going back and forth, back and forth, like when I'm doing crossover dribbles, setting up a defender for my next move. Except I have no idea where I'm going to go.

"You don't know about any of that?" I nod at the journal.

"I know plenty of that. Just not first-hand. Your mother said the most, I guess. She found that going through his stuff after he died. It really set her off."

He looks over at me like maybe he said too much.

"What do you mean?"

"There's something in there about...an affair. It set her off. Your dad was dead, she found it going through his stuff, and when she read that, she said she was through. She dropped you guys off, took off, and no one has heard from her since. Seemed like she kind of blamed us for it, like we knew but didn't tell her."

So it was that clean, huh? She dropped us and ran, just like that? I have to say, I've been with OT so long, I don't think too much about my mother. Almost like, if she didn't care, why should I? Pax mentions her from time to time, like he's giving me an opening to vent about it, but what can I say? I'm just not feeling it.

"My dad never said anything about it?"

"No, he didn't want to talk about it. I didn't really ask either. The moment never felt right, and I just left it. I thought we'd have more time."

"You could have asked me or Pax to read it to you."

"I guess I was ashamed, too—not of your dad!" he adds quickly. "Of me. Of not being able to read. Of not knowing what was in there already."

"You could have asked us to read it to you." I can't say I feel like doing it right now, but if he wants me to...

"I didn't want to throw it at you guys."

"Pax said he tried to talk to you about it."

"Yeah, maybe," he says slowly. "I probably could have handled it better. What can I say? Me and him don't have the same easygoing relationship that we do."

I'm thinking, we have an easygoing relationship? I call you Old Testament for a reason.

"You said Pascal is reading it?" he asks.

"More like studying it," I say. "He's making notes and everything."

I already ratted Pax out, so I have no reason to hold back now. Besides, he's another secret keeper. He could have tried harder to get OT to talk.

"He read it all the way through?"

"I don't know. It sounds like he's moving on. He might even be planning on doing something to make up for the mess he thinks Dad made."

OT's back stiffens and he sits up straight. Now I may have said too much.

"Your dad didn't make a mess. That was a mess." He points to the beat-up journal on the carpet. "That messed him up. That messed us up."

He's starting to go off. It makes me feel kind of uncomfortable because it's not like him to show much emotion. I could probably count the times on my hand, some of the few being how he cried when they put my dad and my gram into the ground.

"But why did he write all that stuff and leave it for someone else to find it?" I ask. "I mean, he could have burnt it. And no one would have known any of this stuff."

"I don't know and I'm not gonna judge him now." He sighs. "You don't know the story, but it was strange how it all went down. He signed up right after nine--eleven. He wanted to go on active duty but your mother talked him out of it. How could he do that, a married guy with a young kid? So he joined the Reserves. But the war changed pretty fast. We took the Taliban out, then we moved on to the next country. No one talked about Afghanistan anymore, but we kept sending people there. It just never ended. He got called up and went over, five years after the attacks. And now we're talking about starting another round."

"Yeah, it's still a mess."

"Now you think Pascal is gonna get all tied up in that, too?"

"I don't know."

He folds his arms across his chest, like he's studying me to see if I'm holding back. Which pisses me off, because he's the one who's been holding out.

"Maybe."

"He's a man now, so it's his call. But the thing with the military is, it's not a democracy. You don't decide where you go and when. You just follow orders. From what little your dad did say, I know he wasn't a big fan of what they were doing over there, how they were going about it. It's not like he had a say."

"I hope Pax realizes that."

"So you and Pascal talked about all this?" he asks.

"No, not exactly."

"But he gave you the diary after he finished it?"

"No. I saw him reading it and I was curious what he was up to. So I dug it out of his desk after he left."

"He know that?"

"He does now. He just seemed so into it, and then he up and took off. I had to know what was up. I know he read most of it, but he didn't add any notes to the part about the affair. For all I know, he quit after that. You said that drove my mom away, maybe it set him off, too."

I reach over, grab the journal off the floor, and put it on the bureau next to my bed. No more secrets. Whatever is in there is not going to be tucked away and hidden anymore.

"You really don't know what else happens?" I ask. "You don't know how it ends?"

"No."

It's hard to believe no one has ever read the old thing the whole way through. Or talked it through either. Not OT, not my mother, maybe not even Pax. Talked about things being messed up. That's the most messed up of all.

It makes me think of Post Malone's "Other Side." My dad's gone, and I've got all these questions, more now than ever, but he's not around to answer them. His journal is all that's left.

Fourteen

The ball spins in the air, heading straight for its target. Then a burst of wind rushes up the hill and pushes it off course. The ball ricochets off the rim and hits the chain link fence at the side of the court with a crash.

Pax added a note to my dad's next entry, so at least I know he didn't quit reading:

Bronze Star huh? What did you do to get it? You sure haven't described anything especially heroic in here.

The wind blowing my basketball around is not something you'd see on an indoor court like at the Y. But I'd rather be out here than meet with Wick today. Regardless of the weather.

I think about what my dad wrote as I go to retrieve my ball:

Waiting on flight back to my unit.
Ate in mess hall here at base. Tile floor, linen table cloth, stainless steel cutlery. Everything so fresh and clean. Feels strange.

Went to see medics—decided to have my sores checked. Took a shower. Boy I was dirty. It felt good to be clean again.

Medics said sores are from blocked sweat glands. They will clear up if I keep them clean, cool, and dry. Good luck with that in the Korengal.

Jenny sent me a picture of herself at the beach. Boy it was one that got to me and broke through this mental barrier I have about her. I dreamt about her twice in the same night. The picture wasn't as good as the other ones she sent me but it hit a nerve or something. I miss her again. I miss home.

Got a letter from Mother—I really enjoy her letters the most. Wrote her a long letter back. Sent some pictures home.

Got word I'm going back to KOP as expected.

Went to EM Club at night—had too much to drink and got lost on the way back. For a moment I thought I was in a prison camp.

Saw John Timson and got some news. Smitty and Johnny Lee killed.

Did nothing all day.

At night just laid around and went to sleep eventually.

Watched football game and read. At night listened to old tunes on radio. Another boring day.

Almost forgot—got my Bronze Star.

I gather the ball and go back to my spot at the top of the key, taking a breath before I launch another one, calming myself down to make sure my technique is spot on. The chill wind is making my eyes water, but I shake it off and maintain my focus on the rim. At least the sun isn't an issue. It's hiding behind a dirty sky so it's no threat to my vision.

Playing here this week, shooting against the wind that always seems to be coming up the hill, has been great training. I can feel my shooting form getting better and better. I have to keep everything nice and simple. If I add anything extra to my motion, it'll affect the way the ball moves, too. If the rotation isn't perfect, it makes it that much easier for the wind to push it out of the way.

I still haven't heard from Wick since that second open gym. You'd think the whole thing was my fault! When he's the one that came up with the idea of working together, then totally violated it by flopping!

Babyman Maguire can write me off if he wants to, but I'm not going to quit on my own. Who knows, maybe the coaches respected the fire I showed them? If you think about it, it's consistent with the effort I brought to the first open gym. I guess it depends how you look at it. I'll know tomorrow when I see Coach in class. His face is as easy to read as Dr. Seuss and the way he looks at me when he walks in the door is gonna tell me all I need to know.

The po-po have been leaving me alone up here. They have to recognize my dedication because I haven't seen another soul out here all week. Either that or the cold is just too much for them and coming over to harass me isn't worth leaving their warm cars and hot coffees.

My bro kept reading the journal and he kept getting more and more judgmental about it. I get it, I really do. The guy in the 8x10 at our house with the all-business attitude and the military awards doesn't seem to be the same guy I've been reading about.

My next shot rides right past the wind and through the chain net. Cha-ching!

What I don't get is why Pax doubts he deserved the medals. What's he saying, that our dad is a coward and a liar, too? Maybe he just didn't want to boast. Pax should be able to relate to that. He's got a ton of trophies from being a Holloway basketball hero, and I don't see all of them on display anywhere around the house. OT insisted on putting up something in the hallway Hall of Fame, so he let him put up the team pic from last year's state championship. But that's it. None of his individual awards at all. So why is he so surprised that Dad didn't make a big deal about his?

The other thing is, even if they are a little exaggerated, what do I care? So what if he's not quite the hero everyone made him out to be? It's actually better for me that way. Then there's less pressure on me to be a hero, right? Pax would be better off looking at it like me.

That would be too easy, I guess. He'd rather act like it's my dad's fault we didn't get the job done. Like it's his fault the terrorists hit us with the October Surprise. Meaning Pax has to make up for it, so we do have that one hero in the family we always thought we had.

I make my next shot. The ball bounces inside the net before falling through like a slot machine paying out its coin.

That jackpot seems like a good way to end it. I go over to the corner of the court where I left my phone and pick it up. The plastic sleeve feels like ice in my hand.

I might as well check in on Pax. I never heard what happened with that situation he was talking about. I type out a message to him:

Hey bro, can you talk?

I don't want to miss his response, so instead of walking straight home I huddle inside the plexiglass of a bus stop on the edge of campus. I check my phone and see the message doesn't even show up as delivered. And why am I surprised?

Google seems like my only option to find out what the Bronze Star is all about. I just hope no one in the government is getting reports on my browsing history because it probably makes me look like someone who wants to fight for the president.

I get a ton of hits, so you know it really is a big deal. Wikipedia says it's awarded to people who perform an act of heroism during a military action. That's pretty broad, so I next search for some stories of what vets did to get theirs. Judging by the summaries, most are about what you'd expect. Guys—and girls—got it for risking their lives on dangerous missions, capturing a ton of prisoners, killing enemy soldiers, saving people's lives.

One story sounds totally different, though. It's about a politician named Ken Fury, a senator from up in Maine, who got a Bronze Star from serving way back in Vietnam. I know who he is, the guy's got a big mouth and always seems to be in the news, sounding off about something, a lot of times seconding whatever stupid thing the president just said. A big tubby guy, he doesn't look like military at all.

What it says about what he did to get his Bronze Medal wasn't exactly heroic. He was the leader of a special forces unit that operated in a free-fire zone—which the article says means that all the good guys have been evacuated, and everyone staying behind is considered the enemy. So everyone is a target. Men, women, and children.

One day, Fury received orders to capture an enemy leader who was hiding out. He took his unit out looking for him and they came across a hut in the general area. Fury was worried that someone in the hut might sound an alarm and warn others about their approach, so he sent some men in to see if the hut was inhabited. Before they could check it out, a shot was fired and Fury's helmet was knocked clear off his head. What happened next depends on who you believe. Fury says he simply ordered his men to protect themselves by returning fire. But one of his men disagreed. He says Fury freaked out and ordered everyone to shoot up the hut. Turns out it was filled with women and children.

Sounds like a war crime, right? But the way Fury looked at it, he killed a large number of the enemy, and he wrote it up so that he got himself a Bronze Star.

I look up and it's almost dark. The headlights of the passing cars light up the plexiglass around me and I feel like I'm in a fishbowl. I've got enough of a target on my back already from hooping on campus and I don't need to make it any bigger. Time to bounce. I get up and start to head home.

I'm guessing Pax heard about Fury and that's why he questioned my dad's medal. If he got it for something like that horror show, it would explain why he never wrote about it. It makes you wonder if his Bronze Star was legit. Or was his experience more like Fury's? Did the government call him a hero for doing something he was ashamed of?

Fifteen

The bus driver takes a sharp turn before I can get my butt down and I slide across the vinyl green seat. It's cold and slick and I'm surprised I never noticed how much it feels like the cover of my dad's journal.

Maybe it never left my mind because I brought the journal with me today. I threw it in my backpack on the way out of the condo in case I had a chance to get some extra reading in. Maybe I'll whip it out in English class to impress Coach. Talk about a hidden story!

I read the next section before I left home:

Finally back with my unit. Feels good to see everyone. It's good to be back. Ross is squad leader now. Too gung-ho but otherwise OK.

Things have gotten quiet here. Guys say a house in one of the villages exploded while I was away. Theory is, the local bomb-maker made a mistake and detonated himself and his supplies.

Wrote a couple letters to everyone.

Shot clusters off at 9:00. Real pretty.

Had a good Thanksgiving. It was one of the better ones I have ever had. It was not like in the States but I enjoyed it. MREs sometimes surprise you. And I had good company.

Gone on a number of uneventful patrols now.

Getting back into the routine. It's a strange way of life. It's fine though as long as I don't have to pull the trigger. I've found I'm not the killing type.

My bro practically left an essay after this one:

You're not the killing type? How else does a soldier take care of business? No wonder we may have to go back! OT says one hero in a family is enough—but do we have ours yet?

I loosen my hoodie as I settle in for the ride. The wind is blowing like crazy and I tightened it as much as I could while I waited for the bus. With the way it was tearing the leaves from the tree, I was afraid a gust was gonna rip the hood clear off my head. They were leaving in bunches like birds taking off after getting spooked.

When we pull up in front of school, I go straight to my empty homeroom as usual. I'm sitting and listening to Post Malone's "Blame It on Me," watching the door for Coach without trying to be too obvious about it, when Mario shocks me by walking in by himself.

He gives me a nod as he passes down my row to his spot in the back. Where's his entourage today? What, is it too early for them? I feel a tap on the shoulder and look behind me to see him standing there. He nods his head back toward his desk, obviously wanting me to follow him.

I double-tap my earbud to stop the music.

"Mario, what's up?"

"I want to show you something," he says. "At my desk."

"I'm good here. Just bring it over."

"No way. This is…confidential. If anyone walks in the door, they'll see everything. And things could get real complicated."

Another secret! I'm not that interested in Mario's business, especially after he made me look like a fool in gym class, but I get up and follow him to his desk just to get it over with. The sooner I'm back to watching the door for Coach the better.

I leave my earbuds in so Mario knows what's up. He pulls out an envelope and lays it across his desk. It's not sealed and he slides a finger inside to make it open like a pouch. The tickets to the Celtics-Lakers game are laid out right there in front of me. I hadn't thought about the game in a while. And it's only two days away.

Smack in the middle of the ticket on top is a shot of Jaylen Brown dunking on LeBron James. Brown's head is a foot over LeBron's and he's looking straight down on him. I just wish someone had a pic that captured the look on LeBron's face.

"Yo, those are legit," I say, to myself really, just thinking out loud.

"Yeah, of course," says Mario.

"So why are you showing me? I hadn't heard that I'd won the lottery. I actually don't remember entering it."

"You know there's no lottery."

"Oh yeah? I wasn't sure what you were going to do with all those names. Seems like you had a long list. Did you decide who you're going to take?"

I try to play it cool and not show any sign that I give a crap. But even in my mood I have to admit going to that game would be pretty sweet. It might even bust me out of my funk. For one night anyway.

"Yes and no," he says. "The thing is, it got more complicated. My dad says he can't make the game because of work, so now I've got three tickets all to myself."

He slides the top ticket out of the way, fanning them out, so I can see there really are three tickets in the envelope. Three Browns dunking on three LeBrons. The tickets are all identical except for the seat numbers.

"He'd rather go to work than go to the game?" I ask. "That game?"

"He doesn't have a choice. He has to work. So now I have two tickets up for grabs and it's a lot of pressure."

That's pressure? I wouldn't mind being under that kind of pressure at all.

"Honestly," he keeps going, "I was gonna take Lea like I told you."

"You said she didn't sign up. Did that change?"

"No."

That's about what I figured. If Lea was going to go with him, we wouldn't be having this conversation. He'd have tossed the third ticket.

He must see my wheels spinning because he keeps talking, trying to keep me from getting too far ahead. Too bad I'm already way past him.

"I was gonna ask her myself, kind of like a date or something, but that was when I had two tickets. I can't take a girl and a guy, because then the other guy would be like a third wheel. That'd be weird."

More likely he's afraid he'll be the third wheel. But I'm not going to say that. The more tickets he has, the better chance I have of going, and even now I don't want to blow it. So I let it slide.

The warning bell rings. We've got a minute before class starts. Never mind Coach, kids are going to start filing in any second. This conversation isn't going to be confidential anymore. I know Mario realizes it too because he's starting to bite his fat lip.

"Can we get to the point?" I ask. "Why are you telling me all this?"

"Because, stupid, I'm taking you," he says.

"I'm surprised after what you pulled at PE the other day."

"I was just playing...you know we're boys."

"OK, if I'm going, why is this all hush-hush? Everyone is gonna hear that you took me to the game eventually."

"Because I need you to help me pick who to give the third ticket to," he says, then goes into his longest lip bite yet. "It's Wick, right?"

That seems like the obvious pick, but before I answer, I give myself another minute to think. Does Wick really deserve to go after showing me up like that at open gym? And ghosting me since? I've got to wonder, if he were in my shoes would he take me? After what happened, where he was clearly only looking out for himself, I have my doubts.

"I don't know about that."

"Why not? I know you guys got into it at open gym the other night, but still..."

"Oh, you were there?" I ask. "I don't remember seeing you at either open gym."

"I haven't been going. I can't try out because of my gout."

"Your gout?"

"Yeah, it's getting worse. The doctor told me I can't do any cardio sports."

It's the first I've heard about that. It certainly didn't hold him back from acting like an ass in PE the other day. And from what I remember, he was the one that asked Mr. Brady about warming up. Doesn't that qualify as cardio? Whatever.

"So how do you know about it?" I ask.

"Oh, you know, people talk."

"So the whole school knows about it, huh?"

The more I think about it, the more I think not taking Wick might be a nice little piece of revenge. Mario wants me to pick the last person to go because he doesn't want to be seen as the bad guy. You know everyone's going to hear all about that, too. But so what if Wick hears about it? And he decides I'm the bad guy? What do I owe him anyway?

Mario nods toward the door and I look back to see Wick walk in. Next Mario raises an eyebrow and nods his way. It's funny because it's the same gesture Wick made toward Mario last week.

It's decision time!

"Not so fast," I say. "He's been acting like a real prick to me lately, even before the last open gym. It's like he thinks we're competing for the same spot on the team. He's afraid only one of us is gonna make it, and that it's gonna be me. I have a feeling he'll do whatever it takes to change that."

The real bell rings. The class will be full soon.

"Noel, it's your call. Who should we give the last ticket?"

That's when the perfect choice hits me: "Let's give it to Rodrigo."

Sixteen

My phone buzzes and I look over to see a message from Pax: *What up little bro?*

I get up from lounging on my bed and go over to my TV to put the C's game on mute. Does Pax really deserve my full attention? He made me wait another 24 hours before responding to my last message.

I'm starting to regret turning on the C's instead of jumping right into the journal when I got home. What can I say? School was heavy today and the journal is always heavy. Sometimes I just feel like I need some time to chill. I figured I'd scout the C's to see if they're starting to put it together yet.

Long time no text Pax, I send back.

Sorry about that. How you doing?

OK. You're the mystery man. How about you?

Ha. I'm good. How's hoops going?

OK.

Coach didn't make eye contact with me all day, so I still don't know what's going on with basketball. I only had him for homeroom today so I was only in his room for like fifteen minutes. Mario took up all of my time before school and Rodrigo took up the whole homeroom.

He kept bothering Coach about the open gyms, saying what we do there shouldn't count toward tryouts since basketball season hasn't started yet. I guess he feels even worse about how it's going than I do. Technically he may be right, but realistically he couldn't be more wrong. Babyman Maguire has fully infiltrated our day-to-day and there's probably gonna be even more to come.

Yeah, Pax texts. *I heard about open gym.*

I forgot you had a spy in the place, I say.

It's not like that.

No? Then tell me who you talking to?

I told you I can't say. Just pretend everyone is watching you. Sometimes what you see depends on your perspective.

That's true.

So maybe what went down was a good thing. I showed some fire. I showed that I care.

It all depends on how you look at it.

I shake my head and look away. If he's got a mole on the coaching staff, why doesn't he tell me something useful?

The scroll at the bottom of the TV catches my eye. They're calling the Celtics game a trap game. The Lakers game is coming up, and while the Celtics are playing the Raptors tonight, a quality opponent, all anyone is talking about is the Lakers game. If the Celtics start looking ahead too, they might regret it. It's only the regular season, so both games count the same in the standings. Just one win or loss.

Why don't we talk about something that really matters? I text.

Sure. You finish Dad's journal?

No, but I'm getting there. It's slow. Did you finish it?

Yes.

Congrats! It's the first I've heard of someone reading the whole way through. *So how does it all end?*

You know how it ends.

No, I don't. Didn't I just tell him I'm still working on it?

It ends by Dad coming home and getting killed by a drunk driver.

And the war living on, I add.

Yeah.

And you think it's all his fault.

What? No, I didn't say that.

Your notes make it seem like you're going there.

I don't even remember what I wrote, I was probably just reacting to what I was reading. I didn't know you were going to read it. Like you were looking over my shoulder when I was reading it.

I guess he has a point. Maybe I'm doing the same thing to him that he's doing to me. Maybe it's not so bad to keep an eye on the people you care about. I'd still appreciate some intel from whoever his source is.

Why does it mean so much to you? I ask.

Coming up, OT always told us what a hero he was, he texts, and the bubbles on my phone tell me he's just getting started, so I wait for his next message. *I don't really remember him like that. And the journal doesn't make him seem like that either. I gotta know if Dad was a coward or a hero. Whether he was part of the problem or the solution.*

So you finished the journal and you still don't know that?

No, not really. But I'm working on it.

How? You left the journal up here.

I didn't need it. I told you the answers aren't in there.

But they're down there?

Maybe.

What, are you looking for Mom down there?

Hells to the no! She left on her own. And we haven't heard from her since. She knows how to find us if she cares. What good is tracking her down going to do?

Idk.

I look up at the TV and see the C's are down one coming out of the first time-out. That's not bad, but during the break there was some kind of commotion in the huddle. The scroll says Marcus Smart was smack in the middle of it. That's no surprise, but it doesn't mean he's the bad guy either.

Maybe he's frustrated with their play and just said what had to be said. He's definitely not afraid to speak his mind. Then again, maybe he took it too far. Sometimes he has a short fuse and he's always one of the league leaders in technicals. I could see it going down either way.

I go back to Pax: *So how are you gonna get answers down there?*

You remember a guy named Larry from the journal? Dad writes about him a lot.

Yeah. That sounds familiar.

I'm tracking him down. He lives in Tampa. I'm gonna talk to him. He's gonna tell me what's up.

What if you don't find him?

I already found him, he sends back, followed by more bubbles, then another text. *Sad to say, it seems like most of the guys that Dad talks about ended up dead. But not Larry. And the two of them seemed to have a real connection.*

So, what did he say?

Not much, on the phone anyway. He said he wasn't comfortable talking that way. But he agreed to meet with me. He wants to meet face to face. I'm going to see him tomorrow.

You better be careful. What if he turns out to be some Rambo-type dude?

I doubt it. He said he considered Dad a close friend.

Really? Wouldn't we have known about him?

You know there's a lot about Dad we don't know.

That's true. Still, you're putting a lot on this one guy.

It's all I got.

Something doesn't add up. *You don't want to take Dad at his word. Why are you gonna take this guy at his word?*

I didn't say I was gonna take him at his word. But I want to talk to him. This is the guy that knows the most. Of the people that are alive anyway. So I have to let him say his piece. Once I know what he has to say, then I'll evaluate it against everything else I know.

And then what?

The *then what?* is what I've always been more worried about anyway. Whether my dad was a hero or a coward doesn't make much difference to me now. He's dead and gone. But my bro is alive and kicking. I want him to stay that way. What's all this about heroes anyway? Who says we need any heroes in the family at all?

Pax takes his time answering that one.

One step at a time, little bro.

Seventeen

Don't believe the hype, the tweet says. *It's all lies. I love my country and was fired up to fight for it. The doctors stopped me in my tracks. They wouldn't allow it!*

The annoying notification about the president's even more annoying tweet pops up on my phone when I go to check it. I've really got to turn that off—I don't need to see any more of this stuff. Coach hates it when he catches us looking at our phones in class anyway. The only reason I pulled it out of my pocket was I thought it might be Pax. Like he'd get back to me that fast.

Turns out the president has his own connection to the Vietnam War—he skipped it. People say he dodged the draft back then by making up a bogus medical issue and paying a doctor to sign off on it.

My enemies don't love our country the way I do! His next tweet goes. *They'd rather embarrass me than win the war on terror. They're just losers! I'll never be one! If Congress doesn't give me the draft, I'll sign an executive order to get the troops I need and get the biggest W ever!*

Apparently, the president's recruiting effort isn't going well, because he's talking about making some changes. Some are kind of scary, like that executive order, and others sound like a joke. The drinking age is 21, but if you enlist, he'll waive it and you won't have to wait. So sign up and toast yourself with a legal beer!

Coach clears his throat at the front of class and waits for our undivided attention. Sad to say, I couldn't read his face when he walked in this morning either. I guess he is leveling up here in high school, because from looking at him, you'd think nothing ever happened. And obviously that's not the case.

"OK," Coach starts the lesson. "So last time we talked about the elements of a story, and you identified the role each of them played in an example you found. You did a really good job with that, so it's time to take it up a notch. Today, I want you to create your own story..."

The class groans so loud it actually stops him.

He pauses a sec, apparently happy he finally has our attention, then keeps talking over the complaints. "You don't have to write a whole book. Just make up your own example and write a scene that incorporates each element. So what do you need? It's all on the board." He puts his arms in front of the smartboard display next to him like that lady revealing a completed puzzle on the *Wheel of Fortune*. "A setting, character, and a goal, right? What we talked about already."

"Aw c'mon," Rodrigo says, obviously still not feeling it. "How we gonna do all that in one class?"

"I'm surprised you of all people have an issue with that, because the way I remember it, you were one of the stars of our last class," Coach says, looking directly at Rodrigo and nodding the way he does when he's trying to convince you of something. The nodding thing can be contagious but Rodrigo's head, which always seems to be cocked one way or another anyway, doesn't move one bit. I'm guessing he's not feeling it.

"OK, OK," Coach says. "How about this? You guys worked well in pairs last time, so let's try that again. Once you come up with a draft scene, we'll set up peer review partners, where you can go through it together before you do a final draft for homework tonight. We good?"

Most of the class groans again. It sounds like way more work than the first time he talked about it. And knowing him, any other changes will only make it even worse. The class seems to recognize that because the grumbles become more subdued.

"This is the template you'll use," Coach says, updating the smartboard. "Open your Chromebooks and check your email. This form is in there waiting for you. Fill it out to add each element, then in the box below, write your scene. Let's go for 500 words, basically about a full page. You'll be able see your word count at the bottom of the window as you work, if you want to track it." He ends by slapping his hands together. "All right, let's do this!"

Rodrigo immediately turns his desk to face mine. "You on this, right?" He thinks I'm gonna carry him again today like I did last time.

"Yeah, sure," I say. "Mario talk to you yet?"

"Nah, what up?"

"We got an extra ticket to the C's-Lakers game if you want it."

"Say what?" he asks, cocking his head backwards, the exact opposite of the direction Coach was just trying to put it. "You asking me? Why? So you can listen to me analyze the game and see what you can learn?"

"Ah," I answer slowly. "That would be a no."

"Why would I wanna go with a couple Celtics fans?" he asks next. "And sit in an arena full of Celtics fans? All hating on my boys?"

"It's not like that," I say. "I got respect for the Lakers. I thought you respected the Celtics, too. You love hoops, I thought you'd appreciate a huge game like this one."

He cocks his head sideways and looks me dead in the eye. "I know you and your boy got some drama going on, and I don't need to get in the middle of that. We did good on that presentation the other day, but we ain't homies yet. Maybe Maguire will make us all homies this winter."

Fat chance, I'm about to say, when Lea appears next to us.

"Thanks for keeping my spot warm," she says to Rodrigo.

"What you mean?" He turns his cocked head her way.

"You act like the two of you are permanent partners," she says.

"Coach said we're working the same way as last time."

"No, he didn't. We're working in partners again, but not the same partners. I don't know who you have. But I'm with Noel."

Rodrigo bangs his arms off the top of the desk as he gets up to find Coach.

"I guess he really likes working with you," she says with a bright smile.

"Him too, huh?" I say.

Her smile disappears and she goes right into the assignment. "So we'll just work here? You seem pretty settled."

"Yeah, of course," I say, and she takes Rodrigo's seat.

She sits and I watch as her look softens from the serious look she wore earlier.

"Um, was that the Celtics game you were talking about?" she asks.

"Uh-huh."

"You going?"

"Yeah. You want to come? Mario has an extra ticket."

"I don't want to go because you have an extra ticket," she says. "So, how do you want to start? Do you have your story idea?"

"No, I'm still working through it, do you want to go first?"

"Sure, so I was thinking, there's this basketball player, and he really wants to make his high school team. But there are only so many spots and a bunch of really good players he thinks he has to beat out."

"Anyone special in mind?" I ask. It's like I can't help playing with her. Even though I know I'm probably about to get slapped.

"Rodrigo, of course!"

There it is! I laugh out loud. Why would she write about that jerk? Then I wonder if I made myself look like a jackass again, till she laughs too.

Coach looks over at me from the front of the room with a look on his face like he's starting to regret the pairing. Like I'm gonna spend the class acting like a clown to impress her.

"I'm just kidding about that," she says. "I know what I want to do. I won't tell you now so it's fresh when you see my draft."

"Sure, whatever," I say, still trying to play it cool.

"So how about you?" she asks. "What's your story?"

"I don't know. I'm kind of stuck."

"Really, you did so good last time. Maybe you need to keep going with that theme, you know, video games."

"I could do that, but I'm not really feeling basketball right now."

She pauses, like she knows why, then keeps going. "Maybe you could pick another type of video game?"

I hear that. With all the reading about Afghanistan I'm doing, I could do a military-style video game, like an *Assassin's Creed* type of game. Those are usually based on history, with talk of us going back, it feels like history...and current events...and the future, all at the same time.

"What do you think about this?" I ask, leaning forward, noticing I'm even closer now and enjoying it while it lasts. "It's a video game. It's the near future, the president signs the order to get his draft, and an eighteen-year-old kid, let's call him Double X, is the first to be called."

"Sounds interesting," she says. "Double X sounds like a real tough guy. What's his goal? To win the war? To save his ass? Both?"

"Well, he really just wants to drink beer, Dos Equis, to be exact. That's why he calls himself XX."

She laughs.

"I'll see if I can work out the goal as I write."

"Maybe it will help to think about the antagonists. Who are the bad guys? The president who drafted him? The other Army? The beer industry who has now joined the military-industrial complex?"

"Hm, for now, let's say the enemy, the Stanistani. XX gets dumped in Stanistan and he has to fight to survive. And he's up against some real mean bastards. When the Stanistani hear a badass like XX is on his way, they plan to get to him before he gets to his base. They want to ambush him and his squad before they get set up."

"That sounds credible. I like it. So let's take some time to work through our stories and then we'll exchange papers, OK?"

"Sure."

I open up my Chromebook, go to the template from Coach, jump down to the part where I'm supposed to write my scene, and start typing:

XX scans the moonlit valley for signs of life from his seat near the door of the Chinook helicopter. His fully-loaded M-4 assault rifle rests on his lap in case he does and he doesn't like what he sees.

The pilot flies dead center over the stream running below them. The only thing he's thinking about is avoiding the steep walls of the valley. The roaring of the engine bounces off the walls and right back at them so they can't hear anything outside.

Damn, XX curses under his breath. What an amateur! Flying in the center of the valley may make it easier for him to see, but it also makes it easier for everyone else to see us. And lit up under this full moon, the Chinook looks like a plucked turkey ready for roasting with an RPG.

Everyone else in the helicopter is acting like they're on R&R. The fools don't realize the danger that is out there, all around them. They think the war will start when they want it to, like they are going to choose when and where to engage the enemy.

He knows it's not like that. The war started for him when they entered Stanistani air space. He knows the bastards are out there somewhere, waiting for their moment. The moment the squad least suspects it, most likely. Which would be, what, right now?

At least he'll get to drink a nice cold beer when he gets to the base. If they have ice. He's never been to a fort so he doesn't know. He's been looking forward to that first Dos Equis since he signed up. They better have coolers full of ice!

He still has to get himself there in one piece. No beer is going to stay in his body if he's been shredded by bullets. It'll just pour out of him in little streams like water through a strainer.

Or like the narrow river below us, he thinks. His eyes go there again and that's when he sees it. A boulder right in the middle of the river has a shiny tube sticking out of the top. At first, he thinks it's someone in a scuba outfit poking their head out of the water, but as they get closer he realizes the scale is all wrong. It's too big for that. It's some kind of cover and underneath it is a Stanistani with an RPG launcher pointed their way.

He leans into the cab of the Chinook to shout out the danger to the rest of his squad when his attention is diverted by a flash from the tube. The moon glints off the tip of the RPG as it speeds toward them, aimed at the fat underbelly of the Chinook. In an instant he realizes exactly what's about to happen.

He has a decision to make. Does he go down with the ship? Or leap out the open door beside him? In a moment, he reacts. It's a split-second decision that comes from the gut, not the brain...

"All right, time's up," Coach announces. "Go ahead and send your draft to your partner for the peer review."

I look up and I feel like I'm somewhere different, like I just popped my head out of the water for some air after coming up from the deep end of the pool.

Lea is staring straight at me. "You looked like you were really on a roll there," she says.

I check my Chromebook again and I'm amazed to see how much I wrote. According to the word count at the bottom of the page, I've already got more than the 500 words I need.

"My turn," she says, and swaps Chromebooks with me.

"I was going to email it to you," I say.

"Sorry, but I couldn't wait for that!" She leans right in and starts reading. I watch as her eyes slide back and forth across the screen, growing wider and wider as she goes. "This is crazy good!"

She finally shuts the laptop and looks up. "You didn't finish— were you almost done?"

I honestly have no idea. "I don't know. I was just writing. I wasn't really thinking at all. I'm not a hundred percent on where I was going with it."

"Really? I'm dying to know what your character is going to do."

"Me too."

Eighteen

The next open gym is coming up so I decide to skip the bus ride home and shoot some hoops outside at the U to help me get ready. My game has to be on point tonight. If Babyman is thinking he doesn't need me, I want to put on a show.

Too bad my mind is still racing from the story I started in English class and how to end it. I'm starting to think the way to slow the turmoil in my head is to finish my dad's journal and find out how his story ends. What's left is pretty thin and I'd be done by now if it weren't for all the distractions.

I decide now is as good a time as any and park my butt at the campus bus stop. I take the journal out of my backpack and read the final pages:

Quiet season ended with a QRF. Another squad needed help. 6 killed. There was nothing we could do—got there too late.

Another firefight. RPG split Humvee in two. Sheer hell. Dick got killed.

Found massive cave complex. Goose got wounded inside—not seriously.

CO killed. Booby-trapped bunker in cave.

I am going to try to write Jenny tonight. Haven't written for quite a while. Just don't know what to say. I have a feeling of indifference for home again.

Coming down with cold. Sores are back too.

I'm on a real bummer, depressed over this stupid war. Can't see a purpose to it.

Larry got a job off line today—has to go to back to school.

New men came out. It is lonely without Larry. It is real strange, it seems as if I don't belong, I don't know anyone. Everyone is new. I feel lost.

Got a letter from Larry's mom. Says he is going to extend. She is worried about him.

Went on patrol this morning.

CO took me and Goose off line—we're too short to go out.

Got another letter from Larry's mom. She was happy about the one I sent her trying to reassure her.

Another Humvee got it this evening—took 11 RPG hits. From what I heard it was squad leader's fault—but I know it's mine, too. I should have been there. If I was there it wouldn't have happened like that.

I wrote my sister to tell her I want her to pick me up at the airport.

Wrote last letter home.

Still laying around, doing nothing. Waiting to go in—in a couple of days I hope.

Got clearance papers.

Goose left this morning.

Waiting to be called.

Leave tomorrow.

Got bumped. No flight.

Flight confirmed. I get home at 6 p.m. tomorrow.

Thank you, God!

Pax didn't add anything to this one so I add a mental note of my own:

Amen to that! Thank you, God! I'm done reading—and no more surprises!

So that's it. You know my dad really was hyped to get out of there because the exclamation point he used at the end was the first I've seen in a really long time.

The part about his buddy Larry deciding to extend was a surprise. You'd think him and my dad would be on the same page. I can't wait to hear how Pax's talk with him went—whenever he gets around to telling me.

Something moving in front of me catches my eye and I look up to see a flyer taped to the plexiglass with one of its corners coming loose. The flyer is flapping in place like a bird with an injury.

It's just a photocopied sheet of paper, with some hand-drawn text and a peace sign written in black marker:

11/11/1919. THE FIRST ARMISTICE DAY.

REMEMBRANCE RALLY FOR PEACE @ 11:00 AM

I forgot that it's Veterans' Day tomorrow. No school! I didn't plan to hold anything back at open gym tonight anyway, but now I can really go off, since I can sleep as late as I want in the morning.

All of a sudden, I hear someone gunning a small engine nearby, which seems totally out of place. It sounds too close to be coming from the food warehouse where Pax used to work, but I'm not exactly sure. My view of the campus is blocked by the big mushroom dome of the reactor building, and it sounds like whatever is making the noise is behind that.

I need to head that way anyway so I walk over to check it out. As I get closer, I can see the doors to the warehouse are open. That's weird, because when Pax was there, he always got out early the day before a holiday, since there'd be less demand than usual at the cafeteria.

What's even weirder is the door to the office in the back of the loading area is open too. And it looks like it got tossed. Then it hits me—the sound was a forklift! Someone must have broken into the office, taken the keys, and stolen the forklift.

People break into the warehouse from time to time for free food, but stealing a forklift is taking it to another level. They must be using it to load a bunch of crates onto a truck or something.

I guess it's not that big a deal, except someone who doesn't know how to drive a forklift, especially one that's not loaded right, might lose control on the hill and head right into traffic. I get chills when I think that what happened to my dad might happen to someone else. I can't let it go. I have to follow them.

When I take the corner of the warehouse, I see the forklift racing away from me diagonally across a small parking lot. There are two guys on it—one is driving and the other is hanging on the side riding shotgun. And they're not carrying anything but themselves.

It's one of the weirdest things I've ever seen. A forklift racing around the campus! It's possible that they are going to use it to move something for the rally. But they're driving way too fast. Something's not right.

I keep following them past a second building, but I can't see the forklift anymore. When I'm about to try somewhere else, I see a flash of movement inside the double doors of a building over to my right.

I walk up and look in the window. The hallway is dark and I can only see about 20 feet down. There's no sign of the forklift. The door is unlocked so I open it and step inside. I hear the engine further down the hallway. And smell the exhaust. The guys are giving it all it's got. Just what are they up to?

After I slide forward a few more feet, I can see the forklift moving clumsily down the other end of the hallway. At first, I can't see the guy who was riding shotgun, and I freeze at the thought that he might be behind me. Then I notice him waving an arm out in front of the forklift. He's guiding the driver down the hallway.

I slink forward, keeping to the side. The guy in front has his back to me so I creep up to about 20 feet behind them and duck into a stairwell. I get a better look at both of them. They look like they're about my brother's age and they're dressed in T-shirts and shorts. This time of year? They have to be college students. It's practically the school uniform.

The long hallway ends in a large gray door. It looks like a garage door, the kind that opens from the bottom. It has one of those black and yellow radiation signs that look like a mean face on it. I realize I'm in the building attached to the university's reactor. A nu-cle-ar reactor is on the other side of that door!

The only sound is the forklift grinding its way down the hallway. There's no one else around either. It's just me and these two guys in here.

The forklift finally comes to a stop. I hear a loud snap, then a heavy chain being dragged along the floor. The guy in front tosses a padlock and chain aside. He cut the lock off the door!

Next, he motions toward the driver with his arm, like he's telling the other guy to calm down. He's actually telling the driver to lower the lift as much as he can. Then he steps behind him and to the side.

I stay out of sight as much as I can while still keeping an eye on what's happening. It looks like they're trying to position the arms of the forklift under the door, and raise them to bust it off. The other problem with the forklift, besides its power, is the big tank of propane on the back. It's basically a weapon, and I have a bad feeling that these guys want to use it to blow the reactor!

I know I have to do something. But what? I look up and down the hallway and spot a red emergency phone across the way, about halfway between me and the forklift.

UNIVERSITY POLICE.

CALL FOR ASSISTANCE.

I have to leave my hiding spot to get to the phone, but at this point, I have no choice. If I were a little more like Spider-Man, I could walk on the ceiling, but I'll have to do it on foot. I slink across the hallway, grab the phone, duck down as low as I can, and cup my hands over the mouthpiece.

Luckily someone picks up right away:

"University police."

I speak in a low voice:

"This is an emergency. There are..."

"Hello? Anyone there? University police."

They can't hear me over the forklift. I whisper as loud as I can:

"You gotta get over here! There are a couple guys in the reactor building. They stole a forklift from the warehouse. And they're trying to get into the reactor!"

"What? Is this..."

"Yes! This is real! You need to get down here!"

"OK, OK! We'll be there in two minutes!"

I replace the phone and look back up the hallway. The back of the forklift is slightly raised. It's straining to open the door.

There's a long crunching sound and the door starts moving. They're going to bust it off! I have no idea if the po-po will get here in time. Or what they'll do when they get here.

I know I can't just wait and hope. I have to do something. I have an idea, a chance to stop these guys. It's the only thing I can think of.

I take a few steps toward the forklift then start sprinting forward. I get to the right side of the forklift unnoticed—almost. As I appear at his side, the driver turns to look at me, his eyes wide in a look of surprise. I use the time to reach in and grab the key to the forklift. I turn it to the left, kill the engine, and jerk it free.

"What the...hey!" The driver snaps out of it. "Give me that!"

I try to pivot away but he grabs my forearm and stops me in my tracks. So I jab the key into his bicep. Then twist it.

The guy shouts in pain and loses his grip on me. My spidey-sense is telling me to get out of there fast and I spin around, but I'm disoriented. It takes me a sec to find the glowing exit sign marking the way out. I'm about to run when I hear a whooshing sound behind me. Something heavy lands on the top of my head and I start falling toward the ground. Then everything goes black.

Nineteen

My vision flashes from black to white and back again, the same way the lights flicker at the condo before we lose power. Then I realize it's just me blinking my eyes for the first time in a long time. I finally crack my crusty eyelids all the way open and a hospital room takes shape around me.

When I realize where I am and remember what happened to me, I lift my arms to check my head. It's all wrapped up in a bandage and I'm surprised it's not killing me. I know why when I see I'm hooked up to an IV drip.

Pax appears at the foot of my bed and moves his hand to his mouth to shoosh me. Then he points a clicker at a TV on the wall behind him. It's paused at the beginning of a news report. Some guy in a monkey suit is standing outside, frozen in place, his mouth halfway open behind a microphone.

Before he can play the video, a big, bald guy in teal scrubs walks into the room.

"Hey bro, I'm Nurse Jay," he says. He comes right up to me and looks me dead in the eyes. "A little birdie told me you were up. How's that head feeling?"

"I feel...good," I say, voice crackling like my mouth is full of Rice Krispies and no milk.

"Sweet," he says, handing me a cup of ice water with a straw, then hitting a button to raise the back of the bed so I can drink it. "Your brother fill you in on how you got here?"

I take a good long drink before answering so I'll be able to get the words out. I let the cold water sit in my mouth, feeling it absorb the moisture, before I gulp down what's left.

"Looks like he's trying," I say, nodding at the TV. "But he doesn't have to. I know a college kid hit me in the back of the head. With a padlock, most likely."

"Well, being able to put two-and-two together is always a good sign," the nurse says, looking impressed. "You ready for some visitors? Friends and family?"

"Yeah, the media can wait for the press conference," Pax says, breaking into a crazy ear-to-ear smile.

"Friends and family is cool," I say, ignoring whatever my bro has going on.

"OK, great," the nurse says. He takes a small iPad from one of the front pockets of his scrubs and jabs at it with his thumbs. "I'll let everyone know," he says, then heads out.

"You gonna play that or what?" I ask Pax.

"Oh yeah," he answers, still smiling.

I take another drink and ease my head back against the pillow as he finally starts the video. The TV reporter is set up in front of the U's nuclear reactor. He's speaking in a loud and dramatic voice, like he's giving a big story the respect it deserves:

I'm here with the latest developments on the attempt by two University of Holloway students to breach the core of the university's research reactor last evening. The students allegedly broke into the reactor with a forklift and planned to detonate the propane-fueled vehicle inside.

It was one of a series of similar small-scale attacks around the country. Poorly planned and hastily carried out, the attacks appear to be an effort by the president's supporters to demonstrate the threat terrorists pose to the country and the need to augment the military. *Experts say the foiled attacks and their obvious motivation will likely end all talk of the draft. The investigation into the attacks is reportedly nearing its conclusion but the perpetrator—foreign or domestic—has not yet been publicly identified.*

While yesterday's plans were amateurish, the threat was real. The students apparently hoped the explosion would unleash a dirty bomb and release enough radiation to contaminate the campus and the nearby downtown Holloway area.

According to experts, if the plan had worked, the impact may have been severe. Anyone contaminated by the radiation would suffer from nausea, vomiting, a weakened immune system, and an increased risk of cancer. And future generations would face these same dangers as well as an increased risk of birth defects.

University officials expressed skepticism about the plan's chances of success, insisting the nuclear engineering program's reactor is fueled by low-grade uranium. However, one anonymous city source told us even a seemingly insignificant leak may have contaminated the area for decades to come.

Of course, students were understandably alarmed. A Veterans' Day peace rally on the university common scheduled for today was expected to draw hundreds to thousands of students. Organizers quickly canceled the rally after hearing of events.

So what stopped the disaster? We now know the plan was foiled by fifteen-year-old Noel Prince. Noel, who lives nearby, was apparently on his way home from school when he found the food warehouse at the university broken into and its forklift stolen. He spotted the thieves and followed them to the reactor building. From there he alerted university police. Afraid the police wouldn't arrive in time to stop the attack, Noel took matters into his own hands. He stole the forklift's key from its ignition and was knocked unconscious by the driver when he tried to make an escape with it.

University police arrived just after the teen was struck down.

He was immediately taken to Holloway General Hospital where he remains under observation.

Pax kills the TV and walks over to me.

"What, you're my observer?" I ask, my voice still crackling. "I'm just glad you're not my emergency contact. It takes you days to get back to people."

"Easy for you to say," he says, and laughs. "It's hard to believe in less than a day we went from a single questionable hero to two legitimate ones."

"Two heroes? So Dad..."

"Yeah. Turns out OT is right, Dad is a hero after all. He saved his buddy Larry's ass over there. He told me the story when we met the other day."

He comes over and refills my cup.

"And?"

"Larry said the base was getting hammered by mortars one night and he freaked out. He jumped in a Humvee and took off. He hit an IED and it knocked him sideways. Lucky for him, Dad followed. He got to him just as the Taliban did, somehow fighting them all off by himself, and got Larry back to the outpost."

"And you believe it?"

"Yeah, I do. He seemed genuinely grateful for what Dad did, to this day. He even tried to pay it back by signing up for another tour, so he could save someone's life like Dad did his."

"Then why didn't Dad write about it?"

"Larry didn't have permission to leave the base. He should have been charged with desertion. Dad probably thought he was helping him out by not making too big a deal of it. The squad leader got Dad the hardware, but he played it cool, too, to protect Larry. The bottom line is, Dad's Bronze Star is for real."

Now I feel my own smile cracking across my dry lips.

"Yup, Dad beat you to it. But you got there, too," he says.

I take an even longer drink then force down a big gulp when Wick walks in the door.

Ugh. Some hero, huh? Do heroes betray their friends?

He comes right over anyway and, without a moment's hesitation, gives me a highly enthusiastic thumb-lock bro shake. He even wraps an arm around my shoulder in a mini-hug.

"Look at my boy, the savior!"

"I don't know about that," I say.

"Say what?" he asks. "Where did all this modesty come from? You've been walking around like you thought you were a savior as long as I've known you."

I feel myself set my jaw, not sure what to say.

"I'm glad you're all right," he says. "We didn't know what to think about you skipping open gym last night."

"Skipping it? What do you mean?"

"Hey, it's no big deal. You had a legit excuse. You were up here in your hospital room."

"What day is it?"

"Wednesday," Pax answers. "You've been out for a while."

Ouch! I missed open gym, and if it's Wednesday, that means the Celtics-Lakers game is tonight. I won't be making that either.

"Hey, Wick," I say, ready to offer him what is rightfully his anyway. "Mario has a ticket for you to the game tonight. If he gives you a hard time, tell him you can have mine. I'm obviously not going anywhere anytime soon."

"Me neither," Wick says. "I planned on watching the game from here. You know the C's are about to straighten their season out."

I'm too surprised to answer. Skipping that game is outright whacked-out.

"If that's all right?" he asks.

"Yeah, of course," I say. It looks like I got off the hook easy, then I start to doubt it when I can see he's still thinking. "What is it?"

"If you're up for more company, I've got a couple other kids who'd like to see you." He takes out his phone, plays with it, then turns the screen to me and puts it right in my grill.

The phone is open to FaceTime and Old School and Boyd fill the screen. They're squeezed into the frame, so tight it looks like they're joined at the head. Except that one is black and the other white, one has a high-top fro and the other has no hair whatsoever.

"There's the hero!" Boyd says.

"Just cuz I'm your hero doesn't mean I'm everybody's hero," I tell him. It's gotta be the first time I've seen him since the summer. And the lack of sun is not exactly doing wonders for his dome. "Is it possible that you got even balder?"

He laughs and pats his scalp. "Nope, I just got better at polishing it. If you got it, flaunt it, right?"

Everyone else laughs and I add a painful one of my own.

Boyd silences us with his next line. "So I guess this is how it was for Brian, huh?"

I almost forgot about the kid from the Heat he put in a hospital room in our last season at the Y. That's hard to believe, because it's the thing that brought us all together.

"Yeah," Old School says. "But he healed up right and so will Noel."

I scrutinize him next. "You're still working on that high top?" I ask.

"I'm not quitting till it makes me six feet tall."

"You serious? You won't be able to stand up," I say. "The weight will be too much for your teeny little body. It'll bend you over like an old man, and you'll end up even shorter."

Everyone laughs again as I settle for a coughing fit. I take another long drink and ease my head back.

"Pax, that you?" Old School asks. Wick backs the phone up so he can see more of the room. "What are you up to these days? I thought you'd be ballin' at some college or another by now."

"Maybe if he had a real high school coach," I add.

"Really?" Pax asks. "What if my coach helped me find something better?"

"The only thing better than that would be the NBA," I say, my pipes finally feeling good.

"Yeah?" he asks. "How about the G-League? That's one step below the NBA, so it's gotta be better than D1, right?"

"You're going pro?" Wick exclaims. "That's sick!"

"Coach Maguire got me a tryout with a G-League team down in Florida. The Lakeland Magic. They liked me enough to offer me a contract and I signed it on the spot."

Wick gives him dap as Old School and Boyd let him hear it. He wasn't lying when he said he was taking care of business down there.

"It's not that big of a deal, really," Pax says. "I signed for the minimum. It's actually less money than I'd make if I stayed at the U warehouse and worked full-time. There are a lot of perks, though. I get to work out at the Orlando Magic facility and everything. I met some of the guys already."

"Sounds like a big deal to me," I say. "So why does something like that have to be a secret?"

"I didn't want to get everyone's hopes up. Even Maguire told me it was a long shot. Besides, you know I had other business down there, too."

Wick hangs a little longer before taking off. I tell him he can stay, but he says the doctor won't let him come back to watch the game tonight if he overstays his welcome now. Old School and Boyd say they have a workout anyway.

After they go, a blonde lady in a white lab coat walks in. She approaches my bed slowly with her hands in her pockets.

"Good to see you again," she says. "Remember me?"

I'm feeling good, but I have no memory of meeting her. And I feel like I would, because she's kind of cute for an older lady. It's a little concerning, because it means I may not be 100% after all!

"Doctor..." I start, hoping she'll fill in the rest.

"Nice try." She laughs, showing off teeth as white as her jacket. "That was kind of a trick question. I've been in a few times, but this is the first time you've been awake. I'm just trying to assess how agile you are. You did a good job with that."

"So you were trying to trick me?" I ask, touching my bandaged head to remind her of my piteous condition.

She steps closer and gives my arm a pinch. I guess that's what I get for playing with a doctor.

"Sorry," I say.

"No need to apologize," she says. "That was another test. I have to check your pain response."

She sure seems to be enjoying these tests of hers! And I thought doctors took an oath to do no harm!

"How are you feeling in general?" she asks.

"Fine," I say.

"Make sure you let us know if that changes," she says. "You didn't break anything, but you have a concussion, and that could be serious."

"I know," I say. And I do. We went over concussions in our first PE class with Mr. Brady. I don't have any nausea, blurry vision, brain fog, or any of that other stuff, so I'm thinking I'll be all right.

"Overall, you're doing really well," she says, pulling out her own iPad and typing away at it. "We're going to keep you over at least one more night as a precaution, but that might be it. If you continue like this, you shouldn't be here too much longer."

"I can handle it," I say, settling back against my pillow.

"I'm sure," she says with a quick smile. "So, you care for more company? I need to get your grandfather up to speed, but I can send him in once I do."

"Definitely."

She heads out and after a few minutes OT and Coach join the party.

OT comes over first, gives my shoulder a squeeze, and blinks hard. Coach looks pretty stressed too, like the last thing he needs is another concussed kid in a hospital room.

"Looks like good things always come in threes, huh?" Coach pivots. "We heard everything—the city is safe, Noel's prognosis is excellent, and Pascal is going to be the first kid from Holloway to play pro ball."

Me and Pax just sit back and bask in the good news.

Of course, since Coach is a teacher, it's not all good news. "Don't take this the wrong way, Pax," he asks, "but does that mean you're going to take an extended break from school?"

"No, and that might be the best part. The Magic have this deal with a community college down there where I can take classes in a hybrid format, either in-person or online, depending on where the team's travel schedule takes me. I'll start with the spring semester, give it some time, and see what happens."

Coach and OT both nod like they're impressed. I got to give it to Maguire; he's not totally useless.

"Speaking of school," I say. "Can I ask you something, Coach?"

Coach steps closer. "Sure, what's up?"

I shoot a look over to OT. I don't want to embarrass him, but...

Good thing he knows what I'm gonna ask. "Asked and answered," he says. "I'm all signed up for Mr. Moore's adult literacy course."

I give Coach a nod of appreciation.

"With all these heroes in the family running around, I have to keep track," OT says. "I need to follow my boys' sports exploits in the papers and I got to do more than just look at the pictures."

"I hate to disappoint you," I say. "But I don't think I'll be ready for hoops anytime soon. I'll have to try out again next year."

"You have to be kidding," Coach interjects. "There's no way Coach Maguire is going to cut a hometown hero."

He does have a point. Although it doesn't seem fair to take a spot I might not be able to use.

"If you're gonna give anyone a break, give it to Wick," I say. "He's brought his game to another level, but with an attention hog like me around, you may not have noticed."

"We noticed all right," Coach says. "Wick has nothing to worry about either."

"I can confirm that," Pax says. "And you know my sources go to the very top."

It feels like that about wraps it all up. I've just got one last piece of unfinished business. I hate to ask, but since I'm on a roll...

"So, if you think about it," I turn to OT. "It sounds like I earned a pair of those Adapt BBs, right?"

He widens his eyes like he really does have to think about it. Seriously? Is he really gonna make me sweat the new kicks? Didn't he hear the news that I single-handedly saved the whole city?

"Oh, I got that covered," Pax says. "I thought you knew all the players in the Magic organization get free Nike gear."

Maybe it's my concussion, but it takes me a minute to connect the dots. Pax is gonna get free Nike gear...we're about the same height... we're the same shoe size...he's gonna give me a pair of Adapt BBs!

Still, it's something someone in my condition has to confirm. "So...you're going to get me some of those sweet kicks?"

"What did you think this whole thing was about?" He laughs.

"A likely story, I'm sure." Coach says. "How about this turn of events, huh? Between you and your dad, you've got two heroes in the family now."

OT and Pax answer together: "And counting..."

Meet Chris Boucher

Chris Boucher lives just north of Boston with his wife and sons. He is passionate about basketball, learning, and writing. While his hoops skills remain on the amateur side, he has worked to earn Master's degrees in Education and Creative Writing to improve there. You can find him online at chrisboucher.net.

Other Works From The Pen Of

Chris Boucher

Pivot Move - After his dad abandons him, and his curly brown mop follows, Boyd longs to run, too. Or can he find a better way to pivot?

Letter to Our Readers

Enjoy this book?

You can make a difference.

As an independent publisher, Wings ePress, Inc. does not have the financial clout of the large New York publishers. We can't afford large magazine spreads or subway posters to tell people about our quality books.

But we do have something much more effective and powerful than ads. We have a large base of loyal readers.

Honest reviews help bring the attention of new readers to our books.

If you enjoyed this book, we would appreciate it if you would spend a few minutes posting a review on the site where you purchased this book or on the Wings ePress, Inc. webpages at: https://wingsepress.com/

Thank You

Visit Our Website

For The Full Inventory
Of Quality Books:

Wings ePress.Inc
https://wingsepress.com/

Quality trade paperbacks and downloads
in multiple formats,
in genres ranging from light romantic comedy
to general fiction and horror.
Wings has something for every reader's taste.
Visit the website, then bookmark it.
We add new titles each month!

Wings ePress Inc.
3000 N. Rock Road
Newton, KS 67114

CPSIA information can be obtained
at www.ICGtesting.com
Printed in the USA
LVHW080528160522
718816LV00013B/1408

9 781613 095317